Summerfield 4:

Spring Break

By

Lazette Gifford

SUMMERFIELD 4: SPRING BREAK
A Conspiracy of Authors Publication
www.aconspiracyofauthors.com
Copyright © 2021, Lazette Gifford
ISBN: 978-1-955487-01-6
Cover Art: Copyright © 2021, Lazette Gifford

First Print Edition, April, 2021

TABLE OF CONTENTS

CHAPTER 1

I have a problem with the weather. Well, not a problem precisely created by me, but the trouble manifests where I am since I am linked to fae clans and an unhappy ancient god of storms.

The inclement -- not to say unnatural -- weather had started with a summer storm last year (dropping trolls in Omaha), went on to a massive autumn ice storm (which brought an unhappy fae prince), passed into winter blizzards (the Fae's Winter Court), and now lurked nearby as we headed back to warmer days. I often watched the sky and hoped for the best.

Like that had worked so far.

Spring had arrived in Omaha, though, and welcome for the 'at least it's above freezing' warmth and not as many storms as we'd had during the winter. My fae friends were learning to temper their magical outbursts, which had been part of the trouble. They also monitored anything Dagon, the Assyrian God of Storms, tossed our way. He tested my resolve to remain in place as Summerfield, Lord of the Earth Realm -- at least that was my title at the fae court. Unfortunately, that title and the power had unsettled the ancient God.

In what used to pass for my 'real' life, I was also the chief reporter for Wolton World News -- or Woo Woo News, as we all called it these days. We were the world's top paranormal newspaper, which is saying something. Julia, my boss, remains adamant that our reports stay factual. Even around Omaha, enough odd happenings were going on -- and not all of them associated with the Fae -- to keep us busy.

This was a Saturday, and I had two significant events on my agenda for the day. As things went for a Fae Lord, this didn't look so bad. Except that those events were ... well, troubling.

The first was an invitation to tea with the Fae Queen.

The second was dinner with my five sisters.

I wasn't certain which of them worried me more.

I hadn't seen the Queen of the Fae since the Winter Solstice gathering that I'd hosted. That had been an unsettling little occasion, which included several assassination attempts. I had taken wounds -- but they had been trying to kill her. Not a good way to start my official role as a Fae Lord, never mind one who wasn't Fae.

I didn't know why she asked me to tea today. I was nervous, and my fae companions had become unsettled since the summons. Even Brandis, the Dragon Clan's Warlord, looked uneasy. Tessa had started pacing. He would be my companion since the invitation made a point of saying Tessa should be my single guard.

Why was I being called to the meeting? I would meet her on the borderlands between Fae and human realms. I had yet to go to the fae lands themselves, and I didn't mind since I had more enemies there than I liked to consider.

Tessa and I dressed for the occasion in my official colors

of green fields, blue skies, and golden flowers worked into a subtle array. Tessa looked good. I hoped to pull it off half as well.

We could walk into any sort of trouble. I wanted to leave Tessa behind, but I couldn't tell him to remain since she had invited him. Besides, Tessa was my usual guard. He'd wandered into many problems with me in the past, and we knew how each other reacted.

I thought he looked less nervous now that we were ready to go. I tried to copy that attitude. Then I saw him blink and his eyes go unfocused. I wasn't the only one who stopped and waited, hoping the Cat Clan Totem had a vision that would help me navigate the meeting.

A moment later, he took a breath and shook his head. "I don't know," he admitted. "I just see nothing definite, and what I do sense seems more here than there. Here in the human world, I mean."

I looked around at my other companions. Cat Clan, Dragon Clan, and Centaur Clan members had all gathered in my apartment to see me off. I felt like I was about to step aboard the Titanic.

They worried about me as much as I worried about them. Tessa and I started for the door -- but then I stopped and turned back to them. They all looked my way. I was about to say something they would not like. I braced myself because it was not easy for me, either.

"Do whatever you need to do to survive," I told them. The group started to protest. "I know, I know. This doesn't have to be something wrong. I wish we knew -- but I still want you to be careful. If Queen Amata has decided that she's not happy with me after all, then you should be ready for the change. I also have real enemies, you know. Some people might take advantage of Tessa and I being gone, no matter what is going on with the Queen."

"That's true," Kala agreed. She glanced out the balcony windows toward the sky. Dagon plagued us with storms at a whim. I kept hoping he would stop focusing on me, but I made an easy target for his frustrations with the world's new ways. Reasoning with Dagon was not possible. I didn't know what we might try next.

"Don't forget about human enemies. There are still drug lords who think I'm going to take over their territories. There are also Jacobs and Kenwood. They've had enough time to get some courage back and to come up with another stupid plan to cause me trouble. Pam's divorce goes to the judge in less than two months. He has to realize that his past actions will not count in his favor."

"So, he'll do something more?" Asta, a member of the Centaur Clan, asked. She'd started feeling comfortable hanging around with the Cat Clan and Dragon Clan people who were my usual companions.

"Oh yes," Tessa said with a disgusted nod. "If there were ever two humans stupid enough to try something again, it will be them. They'll think Summerfield is here, and since you can't tell them where he is or produce him, they'll assume you are lying. That alone could set them off."

Asta blinked several times. She hadn't dealt with humans for long, unlike the Cat Clan people who had remained trapped here for centuries.

"Oh, and don't forget Gryn," Kala added with a special

snarl directed at her former Warlord. "He might know about Summerfield's invitation and think we'll be easier to take without our Lord in residence. He'll be wrong, of course."

"Dagon won't strike if Summerfield isn't here," Tessa added. He looked at the sky. "Worry more about Gryn and whoever is working with him. Just keep safe."

Nods.

I started for the door again. Then I stopped and turned back, winning a frustrated sigh from Tessa and a few smiles around the room.

I did something I had refrained from in most cases. "I am Lord Summerfield," I said aloud. Tessa gave me a worried glance. He knew I didn't throw that title out there on a whim. "And I order you, as your Lord, to do everything you can to keep yourselves safe if you need to."

"Summerfield." Tessa sighed with frustration.

"Should I have not said so?" I asked, looking at him.

His eyes went odd once more. He seldom got visions, and two in such short order meant all kinds of trouble. He looked at me and shook his head. "Maybe it was wise to say. And I know you don't have to tell the others to look after you."

That sounded like I would soon have trouble. Or maybe not. We'd had a few odd attacks over the last months of winter. Spring had come, and things seemed better. Maybe Tessa just thought about the danger he might walk into with me.

"Tessa --"

"We don't want to be late," he said and urged me toward the door and all the way out into the hall before I could think to say more.

We were running behind time. So much so that Tessa herded me to the elevator instead of the stairs. Gremlins had followed us that far -- little green creatures who were invisible to everyone but the Fae and me. I sent them back to the apartment before they caused trouble.

Kala and Brandis followed us, and I did not order them back. We had no trouble heading through the building and to the children's castle we'd built inside the former garage. It was a nice safe place for the kids who lived in the apartment building, and it held a secret for my people. Behind the back wall stood a magical doorway to other places.

There were dangers associated with that portal placed in human lands, but a necessary tool for my people. We'd had too much trouble of late, and even I'd felt that something worse waited on the horizon. Tessa's visions, which he couldn't quite decipher, didn't help. What if going to the Queen was a bad idea?

No choice.

Brandis took down the magic that kept the portal hidden on our side. He still didn't look any happier about our journey.

"One more thing," I said. All three of my fae companions straightened, and I could see rebellion in their faces. I lifted a hand for calm. "Just remember that I have dinner with my sisters tonight. If I am running late, do whatever you can to keep them placated. I'll do everything I in my power to make sure that I do not miss that gathering."

Oh, they believed I wouldn't miss that one. Why had the Queen and the Unholy Five decided they all had to see me on the same day? What kind of game was Karma playing with me this time? I'd done little out of the ordinary, even for a human, let alone a fae lord, since the Winter Court. We all wanted quiet.

Tessa looked at me. I nodded. Brandis and Kala moved up closer in case anything leapt through. We'd had trouble in the portal before, so this wasn't just unwarranted paranoia on our side. By rights, we should have closed it down. However, the gateway provided easy access out of The Fortress -- what we called the apartment block -- to reach other places. Some of my Fae had used it to visit home. The Cat Clan had stayed trapped in the human world for centuries, and they still did not have their Key back, which was in the hands of a treacherous former warlord for the Clan. Gryn remained out of sight.

Using the portal might pull him out of hiding.

The tunnel beyond glowed brightly with white light and looked as smooth as glass. The walls curved upward in a semicircle that shimmered and shifted -- not good when you were trying to see if anything moved out there that shouldn't be.

We spotted something. We all stepped back, hands moving -- but I recognized two of the Queen's own guards. I gave a little sigh of relief. Better them rather than some monster.

"We will escort you through," the man in the lead said.

"Thank you," I replied with a blow of my head, and I tried not to think they had arrived to make sure I didn't back out of the meeting.

I knew my paranoia about having tea with the Fae Queen had become unreasonable. I fought it back and gave a pleasant nod to Brandis and Kala. Tessa and I stepped forward. We had one guard in front of us and the other behind -- and yes, I felt safer for it.

The tunnel, though, took longer to traverse than it had to the Winter Palace. I glanced at Tessa with a slight frown. "This is taking longer."

"Queen Amata has provided this link, Summerfield. The distance is farther from the Fortress to the Borderlands than it is to travel within the human realm."

"I suppose so," I replied and straightened my sleeve -- a nervous gesture, but it kept my hands busy. "There are still far too many things that I need to know."

He gave a brief nod and said no more. This wasn't a good time for a new 'teaching Lord Summerfield the basics' lesson.

I had never been to the borderlands or to the fae lands. I had held even the Winter Solstice gathering in the human realm, where my hodgepodge of a clan had built a stunning ice castle for the event. If some fae just had stopped trying to assassinate me during the celebration --

Well, some humans had tried to kill me, too, and come damned close.

I am paranoid these days, and there are reasons why my fae followers don't like to let me out of their sight. Tessa was so twitchy right now that I feared he would go cat at any moment. The shape-changing Cat Clan totem had become my most common companion, and as a result, also the most paranoid.

The guards gave nothing away, though they had their hands on their belted swords. I didn't take that as anything more than a natural reaction to being around me since I drew trouble.

We neared the end of the portal. It felt more ... alive, I guess. The scent of flowers filled the air, and I heard the faint ripple of running water. I relaxed, though I saw Tessa pulling at his sleeves and even pushing his unruly hair back. We were about to meet with Queen Amata, and he might be almost as worried as me. We both knew that she could order the Cat Clan totem to return to the fae lands and disassociate himself from me. His Clan had gone hundreds of years without their totem.

However, she could have made that order without inviting me to tea.

We stepped into ... somewhere else. This was not the human realm, though I could still sense some of my world in the makeup. I also felt the soft tingle of magic in the air that came from the fae lands.

A slight mist gave way to a beautiful glade. I took a deep breath of the sweet air. Birds of blue and green darted through the flowering trees nearby, and multi-colored butterflies drifted across the low-lying plants. A path of white stone led through dozens of flowers all the way to a table and two chairs. The Queen, dressed in an elegant floor-length dress of white and pink, sat in one chair. She beaconed me forward. Behind her, a small waterfall cast rainbows where the light touched it.

I nodded to Tessa. He knew the rules and that I had to go on alone now. Tessa moved off with the two guards. I always relied on Tessa to steer me out of trouble with fae customs. Going to sit with the Queen without him to nudge me -- I panicked again.

I didn't know enough about fae culture to face something like this with any sort of assurance. My people had been trying to teach me, but we'd had little time between one disaster and the next. I knew how to waltz with the Queen of the Fae, but that wouldn't help much today.

So, I concentrated and forced calm into my mind again as I walked toward the Queen. I didn't spend enough time in nature anymore, and I couldn't even blame the Fae for that, either. They'd much rather be out in the wilds than in the city -- well, at least if they could still get pizza delivery.

That thought brought my sense of humor back. By the time I reached the table and gave a proper bow, I felt better. I worried about why the Queen wanted to see me, but I didn't think it was something too dire if we were meeting in a place like this.

"Please join me, Lord Summerfield," she said with a wave to the wicker chair across from hers. She smiled. Better still.

"Thank you." Using my title gave me a little more confidence.

One of her guards brought over a tray and placed it on the table. It held a teapot filled with a vanilla-scented liquid and a plate of petit fours along with small plates and cups for the two of us.

I forced calm and steadied my hands. "Shall I pour?" I asked with a nod to the tea.

"Yes, thank you."

That seemed a show of trust, too. Still hovering nearby, the guard gave me a slight frown of worry, but he left at the Queen's signal. I poured for both of us. She waved a bejeweled hand to the petit fours, and I placed one on my plate. She took two and smiled like a child stealing an extra sweet.

It was a pleasant smile. I calmed more again.

"Queen Amata," I said at last. I held the cup in my hand but had not sipped. "If I have done anything wrong --"

"You have not," she replied and then tilted her head. "I am sorry if I gave you that impression. Be at ease, Lord Summerfield. I asked you to tea, not to your removal from power. Tessa --"

She stopped as she glanced at Tessa over with the Fae guards. I thought she maybe had not looked at him too closely until now, and I wasn't sure if that was a good thing or not.

"I fear he's spent too much time in the human realm," I stated in her silence. She gave me a measured look, the slightest hint of a frown. "I've offered to let them all return. Many times. I'm sorry --"

"They are all where they need to be," she replied.

How could I argue with such a pronouncement? I had considered asking her to call them all home, and out of the danger they faced with me, but I was glad when she said those words. I still didn't know why I was here, though.

She sipped her tea and ate one of the small cakes, and so did I. She put down her cup. I held tighter to mine, despite believing that I wasn't in danger from her.

She had still called me here for a reason.

"I have asked you to tea because I am worried for you, not about you. I am not sure how I can help you with this problem, either. You seem to have some trouble with the weather."

"Ah. Dagon," I said with a nod and what came as a strange relief, given that Dagon was an old God. "I am trying to work out the problem with him. He thinks I have encroached on his powers by taking up the Earth's rule as a Fae Lord. Most of what he throws my way is annoying but not dangerous as long as we can dampen the winds and control any chance of flooding. I'm uncertain how to deal with him."

"He is one of the most ancient deities. There are others, many others, who might have made the same claim against you as well, though. Why has he?"

"We have a special link. When I was much younger, I fell into his temple and drew his attention after a long, long sleep."

"I had a vision that he will cause you some additional difficulty. The trouble involves storms, of course -- but I could not see more. It is not a matter for the fae realm, and my prescience in your world is limited."

"I appreciate the warning," I said with another bow of my head. More trouble from Dagon. Great. "Do you have any suggestions?"

She smiled and, this time, fiercer. "There have been times when Fae brought an Elder Power to face the Justice of the Fae Court. Unfortunately, the Old Court is still a duel to the death between the deity and the one who brought him up on charges. I don't suggest it."

"Dagon and I fight to the death? If that were the only option, I might as well go stand on a mountain top and shout insults at him and throw myself off the peak, saving him the trouble."

"Ha. You would surprise Dagon, at least. But no, I don't

suggest such strategies, even with your Fae at your back. You might consider the New Court, though."

"New Court?" I wished my Fae had thought to tell me these things.

"We have adapted and adopted ways from your world. All beings of our type -- Fae, human, even Elder Gods live by basic rules and many understandings. When they flaunt such conventions, they might be summoned to the New Court. We now have lawyers."

I looked at her with a nervous shake of my head, trying to get that chill away that had run down my back. "Fae lawyers? I have five sisters --"

"Yes," she said and I wasn't surprised to find out she knew about my family. "I wonder how they would do with such a case."

I must have looked as appalled as I felt. I shook my head in mute denial and then forced words to return as I banished the thought of my sisters involved with the Fae in any way.

"They drive me crazy," I offered as an excuse for my bad manners, and she nodded. "How do you handle fae lawyers?"

"Let us say that I do not invite them to tea."

We both laughed. "I am to have dinner with my sisters tonight," I admitted.

"I won't keep you."

"Oh, I don't mind being a little late."

She laughed again, and the birds sang a brighter song at the sound. I had a wonderful tea with the Queen of the Fae. We discussed the others who were part of my small Clan, and she smiled at Vane's love of pizza, which had become somewhat infamous among her people.

"Vane is growing up," I said and hoped that I didn't sound too sad about it. The Dragon Clan needed their totem to be older and wiser. "I'm not sure he'll outgrow his love of pizza. We have curtailed his dragon form from eating technology, though."

She thought I had joked, but when she saw my face, Queen Amata laughed again. We talked of others, including the Centaur clan members who had taken an oath with me at a time of genuine danger.

"I have told them they are free to return to their own people," I said but shrugged. "I understand why they don't go. Roan and Gryn are still moving against me. I can't guess how much of Centaur Clan back them. It can't be safe for anyone who sided with me, and I'm glad to have their company."

"You realize they might work for Gryn, though."

"Yes, I thought it possible. The same could be true of many Cat Clan people since he was their Warlord. I will trust them all until I learn otherwise."

"And hope you survive it."

"That, too."

"I think you don't realize that a fae judges you, not only by your actions but also by the people you keep as followers, from Vane and Tessa all the way to Prince Arinith."

"I have been lucky in my friends," I said and glanced from her to Tessa. He still talked with the guards, and I wondered what information they passed back and forth.

"More than luck," she replied. "The Fae do not follow just for luck. You helped to stop a long war between the Cat and Dragon Clans. You are useful and ingenious. And I fear I must go back to my court now."

"Thank you for inviting me," I said and stood with a bow.

"It was a wonderful break from duties," Queen Amata admitted and rose as well. Then she stared into my face. "Beware of Dagon."

CHAPTER 2

I went back through the tunnel with Tessa and four of the Queen's Guards this time. The lights moved in the walls, and our companions proved no less vigilant than our trip to see the Queen. Tessa seemed more pensive, and I wondered if he'd learned something more troubling than I had heard from Queen Amata.

As though facing Dagon was not bad enough.

That thought brought my paranoia back up again, but at least I'd had an hour of calm sitting at that table and laughing with Queen Amata. I wasn't certain she knew what she'd done for me by providing that wonderful interlude in my usual madness. I didn't even dread the dinner with the Unholy Five quite so much.

Though I wondered what had prompted this special gathering. My sisters and I did not hang out together except in the larger family gatherings like the holidays or the grandparent's anniversary. We had never been close. I had grown up in a different world.

I saw Rose more often than the others. She helped me with legal work when I set up trusts for children who lived in The Fortress and made sure their parents wouldn't have trouble if something happened to me. And it could. I lived in a dangerous world, but not one I could share with my sisters.

Odd. My entire life was odd.

Brandis and Kala were still waiting when we came out of the portal. Brandis gave a nod of thanks to the guards and then sealed our end closed once more.

"Well?" Kala asked and showed a bit of relief to find us back.

"Queen Amata worried about Dagon," I said. "She's sensed trouble coming but can't tell me any more than Tessa has provided for us. It worries me that they've both sensed a problem, but we've been careful of Dagon all along, so at least it's not a new obstacle. I need to get ready for dinner with my sisters."

We had started up the stairs at a good clip. Tessa didn't suggest we take the elevator twice in one day. However, I didn't dare be more than fashionably late for the gathering tonight, and we were running short on time.

"Anything I should know, Tessa?"

"I learned the same as what you heard from Queen Amata," he explained from just behind my shoulder. "Along with some juicy gossip from the fae lands. I'll relate all of that to you when we have time for me to explain what it means."

"Sounds good," I said. "I'll enjoy that more than dinner with the Unholy Five."

No one argued.

Tessa took care of informing the other Fae about the meeting while I showered and dressed. Black-Tie affair, of course -- my sisters wouldn't have a gathering at Applebee's like any typical family -- even though I knew every one of them went there for lunch on workdays. No, no. That wouldn't be enough torture for me.

I needed to get better control of my attitude before I left the apartment. I loved my sisters -- but we did not belong in the same world. They had their lives in high society, with jaunts off to Europe when it suited them. The farthest I'd gone in the last year was a few days down in Kansas City with Glynis -- my sometimes girlfriend -- and, of course, the trip I'd just made to the fae Borderlands. Oh, and to the Ice Castle wherever off in the arctic circle it had been located.

I could mingle with my sisters for a few quiet hours. My work with Summer Fields Forever Foundation gave me a little link into their world since Lily also ran a non-profit. Hers dealt with education, and mine had to do with maintaining wilderness. Even so, it was enough for us to discuss things.

I could feel the release of tension in the apartment as Tessa told everyone about the tea with the Queen of the Fae. I fought with the suit and came out with the tie in hand to let one of them finish the work. Kala got me ready and gave a nod of approval.

"Almost as good as your court dress," she admitted, and I thought I saw the hint of a smile, there and gone before I could be sure if she joked or not.

"I am taking the Mercedes," I announced, thinking I might as well drive something to match the suit. I more often drove the Hummer, but that was because I often carted around numerous Fae. Tonight, it would just be Kala, Tessa, and me. Kala would play invisible guard inside the restaurant. I'd gotten used to a fae doing that job, though I was more than tempted to take her in as my date instead. That wasn't the sort of notice to provoke right now. Even if I said she was just a friend from college, they'd be trying to track down everything they could learn about her before the night was over.

That they would find nothing at all, anywhere, would not help. No, we didn't need that kind of trouble.

Tessa would stay with the car just to keep it safe from any sort of magical mayhem. Sometimes I complain about the Fae acting as though they had to always guard me, but I was not so upset after the Queen's warning. They knew to watch for Dagon and anything he might try.

Besides, I could always count on my sisters as a resource for family gossip, and I was ready for some down-to-earth dirt on a few of my relatives. The conversations would pull me back to normality. That was an odd feeling, as though I had begun to lose touch with being human.

Maybe I had to learn how to work with the Fae and less human. I wouldn't mind being as comfortable -- or more so -- in the Queen's court than with his sisters.

No. Not the way to think about his future. I was the representative of the humans. I had to stay connected with them.

"Summerfield?" Tessa said. He had a knack for knowing when I needed a nudge back from wherever my mind had wandered.

"How does the weather look?" I asked, which was our standard question these days. Brandis stepped out onto the balcony and looked around.

"Fine now," he decided, but with a worried second glance at the sky. "Who knows what it will be like in ten minutes. Go. You don't want to be late."

It was something to realize that my people worried more about upsetting my sisters than they did about the Fae Queen.

The five are formidable women in a rich and powerful family, though. All five went to law school, and three were practicing lawyers. They radiated power, and the entire group in one place could be overbearing, even for me.

We had a pleasant drive through town. The only signs left of winter were small patches of snow in shadowed corners. The temperature hovered well above freezing. Startled flowers had started to push their way up through thawing ground, and a few bushes tested out the idea of new leaves, too.

The stoplights were with us, but that was Tessa's work. While I appreciated it on one level, but I wouldn't have minded a pause now and then. I even took the long way, just to have a touch of freedom before I went into the lion's -- lioness's -- den.

We arrived at the restaurant in time and waved away the valet as I got out, and Tessa came around to take over driving. Kala climbed out then, too. I couldn't see her any more than the rest of the people could, though I sensed my guard's movement as a touch of magic. I had gotten used to that extra perception that I had somehow picked up during our magical battles. The only other power I had, but I dared not use often, was the power of wishes. I hadn't the ability to sustain that loss of magic that they took.

Tessa had learned to drive in the last few weeks, and I watched with some consternation as he pulled away in the Mercedes. He wasn't going far, though. I could see a spot across the street and half a block away that he had reserved by magic. I didn't stay to watch him park.

"Mr. Summerfield," the man at the door greeted me as he pulled it open for me. I paused to smile and let Kala take her place just inside the building, close by in case of trouble, but out of the way.

"Thank you," I said and meant those words for both of them.

My sisters had the best table, of course. And they were all there, well ahead of me and sipping wine. Elegant women, all of them. They'd color-coordinated their outfits in gray and pale blue, with a tasteful array of jewels and not a hair out of place.

Maybe I should have gotten a haircut.

"I am not late!" I took the remaining chair, placing myself between Violet -- the oldest -- and Lily, the youngest. I was ten years younger than Lily, the surprise late child and only son of my more-than-a-little eccentric parents. The last I had heard, they were back in Nepal. I sometimes wondered what my sisters thought of my late intrusion into their world. "So, how are all of you? How are the families?"

"We're fine," Rose replied, and the others all nodded and offered no more. So much for the opening gambit and blatant attempt to get them talking about anything but me. "The question is, how are you doing?"

Oh, yeah, I saw that one coming.

"Me? I'm doing very well," I said and hoped I sounded sincere. Maybe I was still twitchy from my time with Queen Amata, and they could sense it.

Since they would not talk about husbands and various kids, I asked Aster about her work at the hospital. She was my only unmarried sister. She had tried it once, but the partnership had not worked out well. Aster had made it clear that she saw no reason to give marriage another try.

Sometimes, she and I could discuss things in real life -- yeah, like I lived in the actual world.

She had more contact with people than the others -- day-to-day work with individuals who were not always rich enough to afford the best lawyers in town. Not that Summerfield, Summerfield, and Brown (Carnation's married name) didn't take on more than a few pro bono cases, but it was still just an individual now and then. Aster spent a lot of time at the hospital she oversaw, so she had far more interaction with regular people than I did.

I sometimes think none of them quite understand what I did with my non-profit organization. Nature to them was a week on a private island with all the best care money could buy.

It kept them happy. I didn't begrudge their enjoyments anymore than it bothered me to see our parents spending time off in odd locations around the world. Private islands were not such strange places.

On the other hand, I had spent years living in jungles with native tribes -- or out in the tundra helping to herd yaks. I had sat in Buddhist temples high in the mountains -- and traveled to the Fae Borderlands of late.

We talked about Aster's work for a while. Lily and I discussed being the head of a non-profit, which was my official position as well. She gave me a couple pointers. And then the look on her face changed.

"But how are you doing?"

Okay, this was getting odd.

"Doing better now that we're past that damned long winter," I admitted. They all gave vigorous nods of agreement for that one. The server had brought our salads. I wasn't sure what else they'd ordered. I had sipped a little wine, but that seemed to make them all nervous, too. "Hey, I heard Tommy boy got into some trouble?"

There was a conversation that drew them all into a heated discussion. Tom Summerfield was our cousin, about Aster's age in years, but he acted more like a sullen teen. He had gotten into enough difficulties over the last five years that the grandparents, who were the uber-rich members of the family, had threatened him. He didn't even listen when grandmother said she'd cut him out of the will.

"I don't think he takes women seriously, so it doesn't matter what grandmother says to him," I offered. That won snarls, of course -- but nods as well. "What did he do this time?"

"He stole a car," Rose said after they'd castigated his manhood for another round of discussion.

"Why would he do that? He has money --"

"He stole it for fun," Violet replied with a snarl of disbelief. I could tell from her tone that he had gone far over the line. "He thought it would be cool -- and then he set it to drive into the river. A gorgeous vintage Corvette, too. But hey -- he'd always gotten out of any trouble before, right?"

"And?" I said, relishing what I suspected was going to be a fun ending to the tale. I tried to remind myself about Karma, but Tommy had been too much of an annoyance in my life. Besides, he'd already done the deed. Someone might as well enjoy the results.

"He called the firm," Rose said, a piece of lettuce dangling from her fork. "We turned down the case."

I smiled. They'd taken on his cases in the past to keep peace in the family, but that peace never lasted long. Aunt Abbie was sure that Tommy could do no harm and made excuses for every mistake and malicious action he'd done since grade school. I suspected my sisters would not be getting holiday cards this year.

I never had gotten such a card from her, being far too strange to be acceptable.

"Chances are that he won't stand trial, though. Once he figured out that no one would buy his way out of this one, Tommy made a deal to check himself into rehab," Carnation offered with a snort of derision. "I don't know if the judge will go for it. I suspect he doesn't realize how much that will put him in the police's spotlight if they think he's doing drugs."

"Is he?" I asked.

"It wouldn't surprise me," Carnation replied, then frowned at him. "Sunflower --"

The rest of the dinner arrived. I thought Carnation might have been getting to the point of this gathering. However, the food proved too excellent to ignore for conversation. We ate with a brief discussion about nothing more than the delicious steaks and seafood.

The meal wound toward an end. My sisters never did dessert, and I would not suggest one for me. I thought I would survive.

I had just relaxed when I saw a dozen gremlins slip in through the door, almost tripping a gray-haired couple on their way out. The small, green tricksters had attached themselves to me, but they had orders to stay at the apartment. Lucky for everyone that they were also invisible to all but their Lord (me) and the Fae.

They created a bit of havoc at the entry, which looked as though it had become an ice-skating rink. Once the troublemakers saw where I was sitting, they headed straight for me, and I did not want them near the table.

"Excuse me a moment," I said and stood. I headed toward the door. Maybe my sisters thought I had gone to help the others. I hoped they didn't realize I kept reaching down and snagging the little pests along the way. It might look as though I was testing the slipperiness of the floor.

"You shouldn't be here," I snarled and shoved a handful of them toward Kala.

"Who shouldn't be here, Sunflower?"

Rose had followed me.

Gremlins looked at me with abject terror. Good.

"Kenwood," I said out loud, my brain kicking into overdrive. "I thought I saw Kenwood walk by, and I was about to go out and give him hell."

"Oh." Rose didn't sound as though she believed me.

"He's bound to keep harassing me." I shoved the door open, looking left and right while Kala and the gremlins went past. I'm not sure what Kala did with the creatures, but they disappeared, and she went back inside. "I don't see him. Maybe it was someone who looked like him. Let's go back to dinner."

I started toward the table, but one last gremlin got in the way, and I almost tripped. I did an inelegant little skip and hop and remained on my feet because Kala shoved me there.

"Careful," I said to Rose. "It's slick suddenly."

I could see invisible Kala grabbing more gremlins and

shoving them out the door, which opened and closed on its own and drove the staff crazy, too.

I was living in a slapstick routine, and the joke was on me.

"Are you okay?" Rose asked as we sat down.

"Fine," I said. "I just wish --" I stopped myself from saying more, but I knew Kala had to be rushing at me. I lifted both hands in a warding gesture. "Nothing. I don't wish for anything!"

Something passed so close by the table that the napkins fluttered a bit.

"Sunflower?" Violet whispered.

"Ha. What could I wish for that I don't already have?" I asked with a smile and sipped some more wine. Get control! "Life is interesting these days, but not dull."

There was a truth that outweighed everything else.

"I monitor Summer Fields Forever Foundation," Lily said. "You are doing excellent work there."

"Thank you. It's what suits me."

"You and those friends who live at the apartment building with you," Rose added. She'd been to the place often enough to know who lived there and the jobs they did for me in the human world.

"It's worked out well," I said and relaxed again. "Preservation of some wild habitats is important."

No one argued. "And you're happy, mingling your work with your home life?" Rose asked.

This struck me as an odd line to pursue, but at least the Kala had taken out the Gremlins, and everything seemed calmer again.

"You have been to my place. I live well," I replied. Oh,

please don't let that be a storm blowing up out there. "I don't mind having a few friends in the apartments since I know I can trust them."

"Paranoid about outsiders?" Aster asked with a deeper frown. The same look appeared on the others, too.

"Well, you know, there seems to have been a few problems. Drug Lords shooting me. FBI watching me. Extraordinarily stupid reporters trying to ruin my life. I like the fact that there are always people around The Fortress who can keep an eye on things. And yes, we call it that because it is a place of safety for many people who have not had that in their lives before. We try to make a joke of it for the children. We might as well have some fun when life goes this insane."

I wasn't sure what I read in their faces this time. Then I felt my next big problem rolling up on the restaurant and knew that I'd have to deal with it before I could handle whatever my sisters were thinking. Maybe they just hadn't put it all together in one lump like that yet. I wanted to ask questions of my own, but a sudden gust of wind shook the windows and drew surprised looks from all around.

This was Dagon in person hiding out in the storm. I could feel the pressure of his presence and the demand that I attend him --

"Excuse me while I step outside and check the storm in case I need to warn my people to get things inside."

I hurried away before any of them could ask what might be in danger from the wind. I did not know what things. All the things. Any of the things.

I rushed outside and away from the door and taking my stand with the potted pine to my left and Kala's still invisible presence to my right. The storm blew harder now that Dagon knew he had my attention.

"Dagon! Leave me alone! This is not your place, and I'm getting damned tired --"

Rose had once again followed me. What the hell? She'd had the door open, and the look on her face was one of shock and dismay. I sighed. There was nothing I could say, but I was glad to see the storm backing down.

"Let's just get dinner done, shall we?" I suggested and tried to sound reasonable.

She nodded and held the door open for me. We headed to the table.

"I think you need a break, kid," she said as we sat down.

"I can't argue with that one," I agreed.

"You should take a nice, long vacation," Violet suggested and looked hopeful.

"Yes." I sipped more wine. "I'll arrange that."

I thought I might even do it. Maybe head to the mountains and hike for a while. Let Tessa go cat out in the wilds -- he'd like that. I knew better than to pretend I would travel without any of my Fae.

The storm died down as fast as it came up. That gave me some relief. Dinner had ended, and while things had been odd, my sisters had remained calm about most of it, like they had expected strangeness to follow me.

"Can one of us give you a ride home?" Carnation asked.

"Oh, no. I'm fine. Tessa has the Mercedes. I'll just call and have him pick me up."

"Tessa," Rose said. "The guy who reads tarot cards for a living has your car?"

"Yes. Don't lecture me." I pulled out the phone. "Tessa? Yeah. About fifteen minutes? Good."

He knew not to just pull up right away. I at least tried to make things seem ordinary. My sisters were still giving me odd looks as we sent to the door and the valet brought around their own cars, a line of vehicles worth well more than most houses. I hugged each one goodbye, hoping they stayed calm. I had enough oddness in my life, and they didn't need to get any more squirrelly.

Tessa arrived. Aster, the last of the five, was not quite to her car yet. She watched while I took over driving. Kala slid in before Tessa and somehow clambered into the back seat. I waved to Aster and drove away with a quick look in the mirror.

She was talking to the valet. He pointed to where Tessa had parked while we ate.

Just one more point they'd add into the 'Sunflower is odd' column.

"Well, that was as close to a total disaster as I ever want to face with my sisters," I admitted and felt my shoulders relax. "I don't know what they thought, but I'm sure it was a good show."

"We don't know how the gremlins got loose of our controls," Tessa explained as he sat back, relaxing as well. "Vane has been playing with them. He might have unsettled the spell. They're back to The Fortress now."

"Good. My sisters seem to worry about my work. We're going to have to convince them that everything is normal."

Lightning flashed across a clear sky -- Dagon letting me know he was not happy.

"Make them think things are normal," Kala repeated from the back seat. I could see her as the invisibility faded. "Which it isn't."

"And which it won't ever be again," Tessa added.

"Well, I suppose we could tell them the truth," I offered.

"I'll come up with an answer," Tessa replied with a quick look of panic. "Yeah, we can create something normal, right, Kala?"

"Oh yes. Absolutely. Normal."

Right.

CHAPTER 3

By the time we made it back to The Fortress, I felt beyond exhausted. We took the elevator up. I think Tessa realized he would have to carry me if we didn't. Kala even had to nudge me out when the door opened, and Tessa led the way to the apartment.

Brandis was there with the gremlins.

I looked at the little creatures. I'd never seen them look so downhearted and contrite before, and even though I suspected most of it was a show, I still didn't have the heart -- or the energy -- to rant and rave.

"Never do that again," I scolded them halfheartedly. "You know the rules."

"Yes, yes." Small, big-eared heads bobbed.

"Go play." I waved them off to their bedroom, where they had many toys and diversions. We'd soundproofed it. The little things had far too much energy.

They went off to their room. The door closed. Brandis looked almost as contrite as they had, though.

"I was too busy trying to judge if Dagon intended to make a move," he admitted. "I didn't even realize they'd left until Tessa and Kala used some magic to pop them back in."

"S'okay." I gave another wave of my hand. "Go play."

He laughed, which was a rare reaction.

"Summerfield?" Tessa said and drew my attention. I still stood there at the edge of the entry hall. "Tea?"

"Bed," I replied and turned toward that room. "Sleep. I've had enough of today."

The wind shook the balcony door.

"No! Not now!"

And it stopped. All three of my companions looked at me with a touch of consternation, but I waved a hand and headed for my room. I remembered taking off the tie and jacket. I kicked off my shoes. By now, I felt almost drunk. I was just that tired.

I had nightmares, of course. They concerned my sisters -- and the fae coming to rescue me from them and from Dagon.

I woke up and forced myself back to sleep without noting the time. When the dreams began once more, I ordered them to stop. Something listened to me tonight. I slept better afterward.

When I awoke, I could smell breakfast cooking. That put me in a good mood. I stripped off the rest of my clothing, wondering if dry cleaning could recover the suit from the wrinkles, and then figured the fae would have a better chance at it.

I didn't spend long in the shower. The scent of the food became a siren call. I hurried out, ready to face my people.

Tessa looked about as worn as me. Even though he hadn't faced my sisters, the event had been challenging for him and Kala, and they both sat at the table, hands around cups of tea. Brandis cooked. I smiled, but none of us had spoken yet.

I spent a while thinking about the disastrous meal with my sisters. The Unholy Five would give me trouble about it after they'd analyzed everything that had happened. I would have to come up with some reason for my behavior that didn't make them believe I had followed Tommy Summerfield's path and got into drugs. I didn't want to consider what they'd do if they thought that was the case.

"So," I said, trying to break my thoughts out of that mess. "What do I need to know?"

Brandis reported on the overnight events. "Nothing after the storm Dagon began and then abandoned. It's been quiet. I think everyone needs to rest after this last winter."

"They wore me out," I admitted. "It's been almost a year since this madness began for me. I've no complaints about being here with you, but I do hope for a bit of calm now that we've settled into our places."

"I'd like permission to return to the fae lands and visit my mother and the Cat Clan," Kala said and sounded pensive. "This seems a good time since it is quiet here. They know I'm their new Warlord, but they haven't seen me in the role."

"Go," I agreed with a quick nod. "In fact, anyone who wants to return to the Faelands should do so. That's my decree. Just let me know, so I don't worry that something has happened to someone."

"We'll work out the timing so that we have enough people here in case of trouble," Brandis added, practical as always. "I'll work up a list. You should go first, Kala. I might want you back in a couple weeks. Is that a problem?"

"I don't think I could stand staying with my mother for much longer."

That sounded so normal that I had to keep myself from laughing. Wasn't that the same reaction I had to just a few hours with my sisters?

"If you aren't back at that point, I'll send someone in to get you," I promised.

"I would be grateful," she replied and sounded a bit too serious again.

I laughed -- but then I saw Tessa was having a vision. He stared across the table toward the kitchen, his eyes dilated and his face slack. I wasn't even sure he breathed, but a moment later, he blinked and shook his head.

"Okay, that was just odd." He stopped to sip tea, and I waited for whatever news he had to give us this time. He put the cup aside, looked at the kitchen again, and then focused on me.

"I sensed movement, Summerfield. I can't be sure you were there, but I thought it had to do with you. Odd movement, in fact. Dizzy movement. I could hear muffled voices, and I don't know who they were or what they said."

"That is not helpful," Kala replied.

"No, it is not," he agreed and sounded annoyed. "However, it had nothing to do with the rest of you taking trips home. And yes, I am certain. So, go pack. You might want to take some chocolates. I seem to remember your mother loved them, and she won't have had any in quite a long time. It'll gain you some points."

"Oh, that's an excellent idea!" She got up, smiled all around, and headed straight for the door. "I'll see you in a couple weeks."

For once, she dropped all protocol with me as she went out.

"This is good," Brandis said, surprising me. "Some of our

people need to go back and learn what is going on in the Faelands. Gossip outside of court can be helpful, you know. We have no idea what the Eagle or Wolf Clans think about what we've done, except that they've remained silent. Queen Amata thinks this might be a time of a shift --"

"And what does that mean?"

"Every few thousand years, the Clans change," Tessa said. "That might mean internal adjustments, but sometimes it leads to new Clans and a shifting of members. Yes, like the Summerfield Clan, but on a larger scale. I don't feel that drastic of a change coming, but ... this time might have more to do with the human world attaching itself to the realm of the fae."

"I'm not sure that's good."

"No one knows if a major shift is good," Brandis said. He looked out the window. "But there could be worse ones."

At least Kala seemed happy at the idea of going home. I hoped the others enjoyed their vacations. And that reminded me of what my sisters had said about me taking some time off.

Spring Break? College was out. I would not head for any beaches, but I still thought a few days in the mountains might be fun.

But today was not the day to go larking off on an adventure. Instead, Barrin from Dragon Clan arrived with all the paperwork for our latest endeavor with Summer Fields Forever. My current interest was in some farmland that sat next to a small wetland area I already owned. I wanted to expand into the farm area if I could talk the owner out of a good part of his acreage. Farmers could be stubborn about a homestead that had been in their family for generations. As it turned out, the sole heir who had taken over the land now rented out the fields and the house. He proved reluctant to sell, but only for nostalgic reasons.

"We'll name the entire area after his family," I said, pointing to a stack of deeds. "It doesn't always have to be in my name, you know. This isn't about Lord Summerfield."

"Huh," Barrin said and started looking over more papers. "We can make that offer. It hadn't occurred to me."

Tessa nodded and kept at work on his own paperwork, which he attacked with unusual vigor. His work had to do with converting the Fortress to clean energy where possible. We needed to fuel the heating system for the vast building, primarily through the winter, without relying on magic as the simple answer. Tessa agreed, and no one else argued. We all knew that she might break my tie to the fae at any moment.

Though I wasn't so worried about that after my tea with the Queen. I wondered how long she would rule, but I didn't ask. Not right now.

The various clans who shared apartments often used magic in their own places. They would help the humans if something went wrong. I counted on it, given the odd things that could happen with Dagon still testing his link to me.

The breeze blew from the open balcony. I looked that way with a frown, but it felt like natural weather. Good.

I wanted Dagon to get settled somewhere else and stop focusing on me. The trouble at the restaurant last night had been the final straw. I was not happy that he'd made me look like an idiot in front of Rose. I was sure she'd related it all to the other four before I got back home.

Could I wish for them to get busy with their work and

forget about harassing me for a while? Dared I wish it, even in silence?

No. I sure wouldn't say it aloud unless my sisters started interfering in my life again. They'd been that way when I first came back to Omaha a few years ago. I thought we'd all outgrown it.

I pulled up a few investment reports on my laptop. Most of them were doing well. I didn't need more money, but I could funnel it into some of my long-term projects and just let them run wild.

Brandis peaked his head into the apartment after a quick knock.

"Your sister Rose is on her way up. I thought you should know."

Then he closed the door and hurried away.

"Coward," I shouted and won laughter from Barrin and Tessa. I looked around with worry about what we'd been doing -- but hell. We were doing *spreadsheets*. It didn't get much more mundane than this.

I let Rose in and waved her through to the living room. She glanced at the table where we had everything in neat stacks -- and from the look she gave me, you'd think we had arcane signs drawn in blood and a demon sitting in the middle.

"You need a break, Kid," she said as she settled in one chair.

"Tea?"

"That would be nice."

From her frown, I knew something troubling had brought her here. Also, she's not a big tea drinker, so she accepted out of politeness to me. Rose rarely felt inclined to be polite to her younger brother, and right now, I just didn't need -- well, the stress. She was right in that part. I needed a break.

I made some Earl Grey and got some cookies, sitting them on the coffee table between us. She sipped the tea and ate a cookie -- but she must have read the look on my face.

"Okay. Here's the problem." She sipped again. "Tommy is going to get off with just rehab."

"Not surprised," I said. I sipped. Rose sipped. "And?"

"He made a deal and named you as his drug supplier."

"Son of a bitch!" Tessa yelled and got to his feet. He startled Rose. Hell, he startled me. "We just got that mess cleaned up!"

"Sit down, Tessa," I said with a wave of my hand. He looked like he would argue. Or go track down Tommy, and not as a fae, either. I didn't want rumors of a big, strange cat wandering through town again. "We know he's lying. Better still, the FBI even knows it is not true."

"Yes," he said, but it was more of a growl than a word. He dropped into the chair.

I turned back at Rose. She looked a little worried about Tessa, but she gave her attention back to me.

"You're right. We have the FBI on our side, and I'm not sure that's clear to Tommy's people yet. I suspect once we point it out -- and yes, it will be Summerfield, Summerfield, and Brown if they officially make charges against you -- then Tommy might find himself in more trouble. For the moment, he's free until he checks into rehab next week. I believe matters should look different by then, but I thought you ought to hear this from me."

"I appreciate it." I meant those words. She stood,

grabbed an extra cookie, and started to the door. Then she stopped and turned back to me. I took a quick step back to avoid running into her.

A wind gust hit the building hard enough to shake the balcony doors. I spun back, feeling more than a little of Dagon in that one. I would have said something, too, if Tessa hadn't looked so panicked as he watched my sister.

Okay, I needed to get her out of my place so I could deal with any problem that popped up. Dagon could walk straight through the wards around the building, and if he appeared in my living room --

No. I just refused to consider that kind of trouble.

I turned to Rose and even tried to smile, but she had that 'older sister about to lecture me' look. I sighed but didn't fight it.

"Rose?" I asked, hoping to get it over with as soon as possible.

She focused on me "Sunflower, stay clear of drugs, okay?"

Not what I expected to hear from her. That was one I could be honest with her about, though.

"I will," I replied and grinned. This problem with Tommy must have unsettled her. "I don't need drugs, you know. My life is crazy enough without them."

I didn't think she appreciated that answer, but she gave me another pensive nod and headed out of the apartment. I closed the door and crossed back to the main room.

"Sorry," Tessa said. "That one just drove me over the edge. At least I didn't go cat."

"Which we all appreciate since we wouldn't want to explain things to Rose at this point."

"No, no," Tessa agreed. He appeared more frazzled than usual, but he sat back down at the table. "Something is happening, Summerfield. I can't sort it out, though. I don't have a clue what is going on."

Barrin looked uneasy. I couldn't decide if it was because of my sister, working with an unhinged Cat totem, or the growing wind pounding at the building.

Brandis returned, though. Tessa told him the news. I was glad he hadn't been here because he didn't take it much better than Tessa. Then Kala stopped in as well, a duffel bag ready for her trip. She heard what Rose had told me and frowned.

"No. You are not staying. Go. This is just Tommy, and I could handle him even without the rest of you. Oh, don't give me that look, Tessa."

That brought a wave of laughter from all of them. Then Tessa stopped -- another vision. A moment later, he just shook his head.

"Still the same," he admitted. "And go, Kala. Whatever this is about, I don't sense any hostility. For all I know, this could mean that I'm coming down with a cold."

"Tessa --" she started.

I didn't step in. This was Cat Clan business between their Warlord and Totem.

"Tell your mother I said hello and not to go looking for kittens yet," he said and grinned.

"That's not a good joke, Tessa," she replied. She even put a hand on his arm. "We need you as you are."

"I'll keep watch on things," Brandis promised, Warlord to Warlord. They'd been enemies a year ago. Kala took his promise well and left. She'd go out through the portal, so

Brandis went down to seal it closed after her.

I hoped she had a pleasant visit with her family and that everything stayed calm here. Tessa had returned to work on the project, and I wondered if he needed a vacation. Could I order him to go to the fae lands with Kala? I suspected that wouldn't make him less stressed.

We went back to work. The new reports looked good, in fact, which gave me some hope for the future. We were just about to break for lunch when Rose called.

I sighed and answered it. This was far more family time than I usually merited, and I just hoped it didn't mean there was some serious problem going on. She couldn't be that worried about Tommy, could she? Was there something more?

Apparently so.

"Hey, Rose," I said and tried to sound more pleased than I felt.

"Kid," she said. She sounded tentative -- that was not the way Rose, or any of my other sisters, approached anything in life. "I want to meet you for lunch. Down at Tristan's. Can you meet me there?"

"Sure." The little restaurant was several miles across town, but I could do it. Why not? At least I'd gotten some work done. "It'll take me a while to get there."

"That's fine," she replied, and she still didn't sound right. "Kid, do me a favor. Come alone."

Okay, that seemed odd -- but before I could ask, she had hung up.

"Well," I said. "Rose wants me to come to lunch. Alone."

"No way in hell," Tessa replied and shook his head before I could protest. "Just no. I won't go in with you. I'll even stay invisible while I wait. But we've both felt Dagon out there the last couple days, and I might hold him off, along with any other things that show up."

I could have argued. I could have ordered, but Tessa could have gotten around it for my own good. And he would have been right, too.

"We better go, so I'm not late." I looked at my clothing. "Good enough for Tristan's. And you must be invisible there, Tessa. I don't want to antagonize Rose."

He nodded in agreement.

"Just pack it up for the day, Barrin," I added. "I think we've worked out most of what we need for now."

"I'll get some letters ready for you to approve and to go out," he replied as he gathered up the reports. The man was a born clerk.

"Thank you."

We went down the stairs and through the new walking ramp that led to the new garage. "Mercedes or Hummer?" I asked.

"Hummer," Tessa said. I thought he would. Tessa always felt safer in the more massive vehicle.

"I don't know what's going on with my sisters," I admitted. "This is way beyond their usual 'bother Sunflower' behavior."

"And that's one reason I'll be with you. Not because I mistrust your sisters," he said and climbed into the car. I took the driver's seat. "However, magic is moving out there, and I trust nothing. Your sisters' behavior is just adding to the insanity."

"Maybe it's something in the wind. They're feeling a bit too much of Dagon."

"Perhaps," he agreed as I started the car. "We'll have to figure out how to deal with him. We can't keep playing games with the local weather, or something in the system will break beyond our repair."

I'd had that fear myself. I keyed the garage open and pulled out, making sure it closed behind us as I turned down the narrow alley. We had almost reached the street when a black van lurched across the opening, the ancient engine grinding and belching smoke.

I cursed under my breath. Tessa opened the car door and started out. I figured we could move the van out of the way with a little magic.

The driver had gotten out and came around the corner of the van, frowning as he glanced from one to the other. Then he shrugged.

"Sorry," he said and looked at the Hummer. "I'll try to get it out of the way."

"We'll help," Tessa said, though he frowned as well. I just crossed to the van --

Someone came around the side of the vehicle, startling me. I started to nod, but Tessa grabbed my arm and pulled me back. The first man raised a canister and sprayed it into our faces.

Everything moved funny as I fell. I had to fight to keep my eyes open, and I saw Tessa had already fallen as well, and I landed on him. The wind kicked up -- a lot of good Dagon would do at this point.

What the hell was going on? Someone had just been waiting for us to come out. None of my people had noticed, and that was odd.

But the world kept slipping away and back again.

"Which one?" a man said, the words echoing in strange patterns through my brain.

I thought I heard arguing and tried to sit up. Someone came close enough to spray a little more of the gas, whatever it was.

Drug lords? Were we back to that problem? At least they weren't shooting us out of hand. My heart did a bit of a flutter at that thought, but I couldn't hold even that fear for long.

"-- them figure it out. Can't leave either here."

Someone caught my arm. The world swirled and turned, and I wondered if the fae were going to help -- or did my people not know about the danger? I couldn't reach them myself and Tessa remained unconscious. I could see that as they put us both in the van.

We probably should have paid a little more attention to Tessa's visions.

CHAPTER 4

There are days when my life is odd. I can live with things like working with Fae, including tea with the Fae Queen, and disgruntled ancient gods who seem to take delight in annoying me and making certain I know he waited for a chance to make more trouble for me.

However, some moments went beyond the usual level of insanity.

Someone had kidnapped me. Abducted. I knew that truth even if I couldn't put together all the rest of the incident. Hadn't Tessa and I been heading somewhere? Or was that Kala and Brandis?

No one had tied me up, but my body felt too lethargic to move. I must still be asleep because this was too strange to be ... well, real.

We drove for a long distance in this nightmare. I noted every bump and dip and the sound of cars going past as we went farther from home. I had a good sense of direction, and I thought we headed westward. From the surrounding sounds, we were on the Interstate. Were we driving to Lincoln or already beyond that city? I had no idea of time.

I couldn't wake up. If I could have, I would have wished for ... something. I wasn't sure what. My mind went down that rabbit hole for a little while, trying to sort out which wish would help me best, even though I still wanted to believe this could not be real.

People mumbled. The van hit bumps. I heard Tessa give a bit of a growl and worried that he would change into a cat. That might have helped sometimes -- but not if he felt anything like I did right now. They'd shoot him. I didn't want him dead, even in a nightmare.

I wanted to go home to the Fortress and not be in a situation where no one found us again. Tessa needed to come out of his haze and prepare for trouble since I had little hope against men with drugs and guns.

My eyes opened a slit, and I watched lights dancing and listened to the sounds around me. Nothing made sense. Boots. I saw cowboy boots to my right -- three pairs. They moved, which I found disconcerting until I realized there must have been bodies attached to those feet. I tried to turn enough to look up and get an idea of what we faced. My head would not move.

I closed my eyes again because just holding them open proved too tricky. I had to save my strength for when Tessa and I took this group on.

We hit more bumps. The man at the wheel cursed the traffic and idiot drivers.

Yeah, too much real world.

I didn't need drugs. I'd told Rose that truth. Why wasn't the universe listening to me?

We just kept driving. Every few minutes, I tried to figure out what this meant, but nothing fit together as my thoughts bounced erratically from the human world to the fae realm. Kenwood and Jacobs couldn't arrange anything this well done.

Drug lords seemed the most likely idea, though the kidnappers were not rough with us -- and we were still alive.

Maybe this had to do with the Summerfield family. That was as far as my brain went before I lost track of everything and slipped away again.

We'd gone off the Interstate. I knew that by the sound beyond the van.

We stopped. I could still hear things roaring, though not as close. Then hands moved me onto -- was this a stretcher?

"Both. Yes. We can't leave him."

I had to parse those words. They did not want to stay in order, but I grabbed at the sounds and hoped I could trust -- someone. Anyone. I lost track again. They'd placed something over my face so I couldn't see even through the fluttering of my eyelids. Besides, the light -- it was too bright and hurt. I think I made a sound of protest. Another person put a comforting hand on my arm as the roaring grew too loud.

I came awake at the familiar pressure of a plane taking off. Well, hell. I found Tessa in a chair across the aisle from me on the small jet. He looked like he slept, his chest moving and his lips twitching. At least he wasn't dead.

I wanted answers.

I went back to sleep instead. More nightmares crawled through my head. I thought I saw Dagon staring at me, his eyes narrowed in anger as though I had done something wrong.

Tessa made a sound of complaint...

Later.

I felt stiff. Hadn't we'd landed once and taken off again?

Fuel?

My eyes opened but didn't focus until I turned and saw Tessa strapped into a chair on the other side of the small plane.

Yes, I panicked. I tried to get free of the seatbelt so I could check Tessa. He didn't look well, his face pale and twitching, his hair damp across his forehead. And then I saw something even more frightening. Rose and Violet made their way down the narrow aisle.

"They took you, too?" I said with growing worry. "Why --"

My sisters brought a tray with tea and cookies. Behind them, I could see the cockpit where Aster and Lily sat at the controls. Carnation hovered somewhere midway between the two groups, her head bowed.

This had to be a nightmare. I pounded my head against the back of the seat and pinched my arm. Then I stared at my sisters for a moment and repeated the actions.

"Sunflower?" Violet whispered, staring at me with worry.

"No, this is real. Of course, it's real," I said and looked at my two oldest sisters with nothing but disbelief. "Why in the name of every God did you kidnap us? Have you gone insane?"

"No," Violet replied as her face took on a less troubled stare. She looked as calm as if she faced some judge on a case as she placed the tea service on the table in front of Tessa. "But it was more and more clear that you have been inching yourself that way, Sunflower. We removed you from the stress for your own good."

I stared at her in total disbelief. Then I considered the

dinner we'd had -- was that just last night? -- and realized all the tests that I'd failed. Could I blame them for thinking I was crazy? Maybe not. But this -- this was far off the edge of acceptable.

Which showed how worried they'd been about me.

"Drink some tea," Rose said and handed me a cup. "Calm down and just go along with this, Kid. You are getting a nice two-week vacation on a very exclusive Pacific Island Resort. Time to rest and recover. We can all see that you need a break."

Was I supposed to argue with them? Could I come up with an argument for taking me back right now that didn't include Fae going crazy if I disappeared? How long since we had left the Fortress?

Why hadn't they found us?

"Why bring Tessa?" I asked and glanced his way with a touch more worry. He looked pale, and the words he mumbled were not in English.

"Rose told you to come alone," Violet answered and almost made it an accusation. She thought better and gave me a pat on the shoulder like she'd done when I was six or seven. "We hadn't told the contractors what to do if you had someone with you, so they brought you both."

I looked at her with more disbelief, but for a different reason. "Contractors. You know those kinds of people?"

"Three of us maintain the most powerful law firm in the Midwest, Sunflower. We know all sorts of people."

There was a new and frightening thought, followed by the idea that if I didn't get things in hand, they would soon meet another set of powerful people.

I'd have to convince them, first, that I was not crazy. That might be a trick because I suspected by now my sisters might be right. Having dealt with the Fae for so long had sometimes driven me over the edge. Then I had to keep my Fae from doing something drastic. In fact, I wondered why they hadn't acted yet. Tessa and I had traveled hours away from home. How could they have missed our abduction?

"My friends at the apartment --"

"I called and talked to someone named Asta," Rose said with a quick nod of understanding. "We didn't want anyone to panic. I explained to her that we were taking you on a surprise vacation and not to worry. She said she would tell Brandis when he got back. I also contacted Wolton World News and told Julia the same. I didn't realize that Tessa would be along as well at that point, but no matter. We're over the Pacific, Sunflower. We'll be on the island in about four hours, and you can call home from there."

"Good plan," I said. I sipped my tea, and Violet appeared less bothered.

Rose, though, glanced at Tessa. "I wish he would wake up soon. Perhaps some tea would help."

I could, in fact, wish him to wake, but I thought there might be an easier way. Tessa would obey an order from the Lord of his clan.

"Tessa, wake up," I said.

His eyes blinked open. Closed. Opened again with a stare at Rose and Violet that made me fear what he'd do next.

"My sisters decided I need a vacation, Tessa," I explained and drew his wild-eyed attention.

"Vacation."

"Yeah. So, my sisters had me kidnapped because they knew I would disagree about going with them. And you got pulled along."

"Kidnapped."

Carnation stood by her two sisters. She looked at me with an actual apologetic shake of her head. "I told them this was crazy, Kid. But here we are, so you might as well settle in and decide to have a good time. Not much of an option, you know."

Oh, I had a choice, but I wasn't about the bring magic into this mess.

"I don't understand what is going on," Tessa admitted with a nervous glance at my sisters.

"Give me a few minutes with him, okay?"

The three retreated to the front of the plane. I turned and put a hand on Tessa's arm. His eyes had gone large, the pupils wide. I didn't want this to get worse. Tessa unhinged on a small plane -- many things could go wrong. Magic, big cat, panicked sisters -- no, I had to handle this one with extreme care.

I tightened my hold on his arm and drew his wandering attention back to me.

"Listen to me, Tessa. My sisters decided, based on that dinner last night, that I desperately needed a break. You got dragged along because -- remember -- Rose told me to meet her alone. Things could be far worse."

"Worse," he repeated, as though he kept grabbing at words he might understand. Then he shook his head. "We're flying, aren't we?"

"Ummm, yes? Is that a problem?"

"Other than we're *flying*?"

"Ah. Okay. You haven't flown, at least in a plane, before."

"No," he said. He glanced at the window as the plane did a dip. "Why in the name of the Gods is there so much water out there?"

"Pacific Ocean. We're headed for an island."

"Ocean, water -- island," he repeated the words as though he wasn't sure of the meanings.

"I suspect, Tessa, that it was either this trip, or I would have ended up locked up somewhere for my own good, much like Tommy. So, we will take a vacation. It won't be so bad. Rose let the others know where we're going, so I suspect that's why they're not here already, right?"

"Yeah. Maybe." Tessa glanced out the window and back. "Whatever they did to me, it has made it hard to connect with magic. It is clearing, though. I should be able to contact someone soon."

Carnation brought us some sandwiches and chips. Tessa tried to be polite, but there was still a bit of a snarl in his voice. Tessa glanced at the window sometimes and growled softly.

I watched with more care, and not because I liked the look of all that vast ocean. Clouds began to billow up to the side and ahead of us. I said nothing to Tessa. Was this an ordinary storm or something Dagon threw at me?

And I couldn't keep the weather hidden from Tessa. The clouds swept in around us with a gust front and a flash of lighting that came far too close to the plane.

"Vacation. Fun." Tessa mumbled.

"Tessa, no matter what -- you can't use magic or change

into a cat," I said as I leaned closer to him. "We're almost to the island. We'll be fine -- unless my sisters find out about the Fae. Then we face the sort of problem we'll be dealing with for years."

"Damn." Tessa looked panicked, but I couldn't tell if it was because of the storm or the thought of my sisters dealing with the Fae. "You're right. It could change the entire world. I'll trust that we are safe, Summerfield. So, I swear on my oath to you that I will not use any magic for go cat on this journey."

"I accept."

No, it was not the wisest decision either of us had ever made.

CHAPTER 5

The clouds swept in around us, calm and pretty for a while. We all gathered closer to the cockpit to get the news over the radio equipment, but it crackled and hissed, blurring out any words. Lily held control while Aster took a break. I felt tempted to take the copilot's position, but I didn't want them to think I mistrusted their abilities. They were both excellent pilots. I just thought it might be fun.

This was part of the idea of having a few days off from work, right? Have fun. Honestly, most of my life had been a vacation from the time I started traveling with my parents. I had visited many exotic temples, joined in native rituals in remote villages, and learned more on my vacations than I ever had in college.

And then I settled back in Omaha with the rest of my family. That had been a mistake. I should never have trusted myself so close to other Summerfields, never mind to my sisters.

The storm looked magnificent as it swept in on all sides of us in a wall of white shapes and sudden a glow from cloud lightning. Beautiful and ominous all at the same time.

And magical, I feared -- at least in the way that a god of weather could create magic. I felt little Dagon out there, but I thought he must be close. Amusing to think that he had a better link to know where I went than my Fae could manage.

"I have never seen a storm like this one pop up out of nowhere," Lily said. She had firm control of the jet. "I saw nothing about it when we took off from San Diego."

I glanced at Tessa, and he gave a quick nod. Well, it wasn't as though we hadn't had some warning, right? Even Queen Amata had said to be careful of Dagon. Tessa's visions of dizzy disaster made more sense now, too.

For all the good they did us.

The storm grew chaotic. Winds buffeted the little plane, and Tessa looked at me with a cross between a snarl and panic.

"This was not my intention," I reminded him in a near whisper as I leaned closer. The plane's engine roared louder as Lily fought against the winds. "It's not my sisters' idea, either. Just sit back and relax. We'll fly through the clouds and land at a secluded paradise. Everything will be fine."

"You shouldn't lie to a cat. We always know."

Lightning crawled across the sky as though it looked for something -- most likely us. That unsettled Lily and Aster, and I didn't blame them this time. I even turned to Tessa because --

Because I wanted magic and didn't care if my sisters found out.

And Tessa could do nothing.

I panicked. Yes, I had gotten far too used to the Fae taking care of problems. I had tried to keep my Fae world and my Summerfield Family life from overlapping. My parents knew about the clans, having lived in almost as much insanity as me.

My sisters crowded around the front of the plane. Tessa and I moved back a few rows. We settled in with seatbelts.

"This is part of being human, right? This 'oh hell, there is no plan b' feeling?"

"Yeah, this is it," I had to admit.

"I am going to write a manual for the rest of the clans just in case someone else is stupid enough to put themselves into this kind of situation."

"Be sure it's anonymous. We don't want anyone to know how stupid we've been."

"We can blame it on the drugs," Tessa suggested.

The plane swept sideways in the wind, then dropped a couple yards. Violet, Rose, and Carnation had all gone to strap in now. Carnation at least gave me a look of apology.

We had a few minutes of a rollercoaster ride. The engines fought against the storm and would have won if it were not for Dagon directing the trouble against us.

Tessa had strapped into a chair close to me. I dared a glance back at him.

"Can we undo the oath?" I asked though I had figured out that answer already.

Tessa turned to me with a shake of his head and looked as contrite as Aster.

"I swore on my oath to you -- that makes it very strong," he said. "It would require the Queen's intervention, and while she'd do it, we have this problem of reaching her without any magic."

"No other choice."

"None. If we tried, the explosion of power would blow up the plane. If we tried it on the ground, it would destroy everything within at least a hundred miles. Yes, it has happened in the past."

"I could wish --"

"No. Just no. We don't want to pit your untested power, something none of us understand, against Fae powers."

I trusted Tessa's opinion on this one and nodded in agreement. The plane continued to bounce, though. We had both calmed, but it wouldn't last long in this storm. Yeah, I had lied to the cat. I didn't think everything was going to be fine.

Time to get serious.

"Tessa, if the plane goes down, you need to take the seat you are on and strap it on so you can float. Get out the door."

"And into the middle of the ocean in a storm," he said and looked out at the clouds. "Lost."

"Or you can go down with the plane and take your chances at the bottom of the ocean rather than on it."

"I would rather --"

Lightning stuck both wings. The engines died, and for a moment, all we could hear was the howl of the wind and what sounded like unnatural laughter. That would be Dagon, and the sound made me determined to survive.

The engines came back. Lily cursed in ways I had never heard from any of my sisters. Tessa looked as though he would have gone cat out of instinct. I had been an idiot. Tessa could have saved us, and I think the Unholy Five would have been happy enough under the circumstances.

Lily and Aster had trouble with the controls. I didn't want to sit by and do nothing, so I moved forward again, and Tessa still stayed close.

"Let me take over for a while," I said and waved Lily out of the way. She looked panicked.

"Can you handle it?" Aster asked from her seat at the controls. "they drugged you --"

"At this point, that might help," I replied, and Aster made a sound of agreement. Lily didn't argue, a sure sign that she felt out of her depth in this one.

I slid in and checked the readings, not at all surprised to find them erratic. Aster nodded my way and said nothing. They had been flying without direction or altimeter for a while. I didn't point it out to the others.

"Sunflower, is your pilot's license up to date?" Violet asked.

"I'm not sure. Shall we wait to find out?"

"I'd rather count on his luck than his license," Lily added. "We all know that's been good."

I couldn't argue with her. So, I had to trust my abilities at this point.

"We should get below the clouds," I warned. "It will not be any worse than up here, but at least we might see something. And the rest of you need to look. If we spot an island, we are heading for it."

No one even argued, demonstrating how worried they were at this point. I shoved my worry into the back of my mind and did my best to keep the plane's nose up, and the wings angled so we didn't hop and skip so much once we went down.

I took the plane lower. Unfortunately, the clouds had swept in so low that they all but touched the ocean waves. I couldn't tell if we flew through rain or saltwater sometimes, but I knew neither would do us any good. With a few whispered words to Karma, I tried to skim along the bottom of the clouds, with only a faint hint of fog obscuring the view, and still hoped that I might see land.

I soon gave up that hope.

"What would you guess is the closest islands?" I asked. "Ahead or behind us?"

"Galapagos," Aster said. Her hands held tight to controls and helped keep the plane steady. "Maybe two hundred miles northeast. I would say the island we were heading for is closer, but I'm not sure. Turn back?"

"I think so," I said. "This is a monster. We don't dare try to fight our way through the heart of it."

"Honest to God, Sunflower -- we had no idea this was going to happen. If there had been even a hint of poor weather, we would have sent you off with Tommy to rehab instead."

"Very funny."

She gave me a quick smile. My sisters were, I realized, just as crazy as me in their own way. Yeah, kidnapping their younger brother for his own good might have seemed a reasonable idea to this bunch.

I couldn't wait to tell mom and dad about this one. That thought gave me more determination to survive. All I had to do was find an island or get all the way to the mainland.

We made a tight sweep and headed toward the continent, however far that might be. If we were that close to the Galapagos, then we'd crossed south over the equator and might be closer to Ecuador. I'd go for that if we missed the islands --

I glanced to the left, thinking I'd seen something, but --

No, but did I feel a surge of power? Perhaps I had a sense of Dagon in the storm. I scanned again --

Tessa moved up to the opening.

"I ... I had the impression of land, Summerfield," he said, pointing toward the area where I had looked a moment before. "I can't guarantee it is safe."

Good enough for me. I would take Tessa's 'impression' over any other options. Especially since the right engine began sputtering, and we had trouble keeping the wing out of the waves.

I turned the plane.

"Sunflower?" Aster whispered, worried.

"You have a better destination?"

"No," she admitted.

"Go back with the others and get them ready," I ordered and clamped tighter hold of the controls. I didn't look at Tessa. "Remember what I told you, Tessa."

"Summerfield --"

"I might pull off one trick."

Aster gave me an odd glance as she went on past Tessa. He, though, threw himself into her seat. He touched nothing.

"Tessa --"

"Either what you plan works or not," he said. He sounded far calmer than I felt right then. "Think very hard on how you word it."

"I am going to have a very long discussion with Dagon later," I promised. Tessa nodded in agreement.

I could feel a brush of magic again. Damn, Dagon. I didn't need --

But then, in a rare moment of calm, I found the island.

"I see it!" I called to the others. "Wide beach and no lights -- I think it's safe to go down there. Get ready!"

I cut the power back on the working engine and held tight to the controls. Ahead of us loomed the view of sand and two tall peaks, all of it illuminated by the lightning. Perhaps the higher peak glowed as well. Volcanic. Not a young island with that shape.

All that information came to me in a couple heartbeats. My mouth went dry. I had no time to think this out anymore -- but there was salvation ahead. We just had to all make it there.

Closer. I still saw no sign of other life.

"I wish for all of us to survive and be alright after the crash!"

Tessa glanced my way. I could see him out of the corner of my eye as he nodded. I'd worded that as best I could, and I attempted to fight against the painful release of power that came from my wish.

We skimmed along the water with the beach ahead. The engines had died, but we didn't have far to go --

And then the plane tipped to the left side...

CHAPTER 6

I awoke on a sandy beach with an icy wind blowing in off the sea and mad seagulls flying somewhere down the shoreline. There is nothing like the sound of enraged gulls -- a noise you didn't hear too often in Omaha. There are some inland gulls, but they don't react quite the same way as those along the ocean.

My mind was wandering. What did I care about the gulls?

The rain fell, which was not what I had wanted for my vacation. Beaches should be sunny and --

I moved a little. Everything ached, and my head felt one step short of exploding. I just laid there and ignored the cold and the rain, though I wanted to have a few words with Dagon --

Dagon. Storm.

Plane. Crash.

I panicked enough that I sat straight up this time, despite my pounding head and every other ache. I had a cut on my arm and what felt like bruises on my chest. My soaked clothing stuck everywhere in icy spots, and my hair fell across my face. I shoved it back with one hand and kept my balance with the other --

In a flash of lightning, I saw all five of my sisters sitting to my right. They didn't look any better than me, but all of them were alive and --

"Tessa!"

"I'm here," he said to my left. "Just lounging in the sand, Summerfield. Isn't that what vacations are about?"

"Huh." I started to just drop straight back, but he'd moved to catch hold of me. He had some idea of what I was going through because he'd been around when I'd made 'wishes' before.

My sisters sounded concerned, but I waved them off. "Headache," I said. "Give me a little peace. How long since we went down?"

"About two hours," Lily replied with a glance at the sky. Her voice trembled, a sound I had never heard before. "We gathered what we could grab and got to the shore. If we can just wait out the night -- I think we'll have luck with finding ... something."

"Yeah. Good." I wanted to sleep through this damned headache and hope that tomorrow would be better. I didn't even care about the sand, the storm, and the cold anymore. My sisters had survived. Tessa was here. I could trust them to handle things for a while.

I hoped the new day brought less rain and some sign of habitation. Rescue. Rescue would be lovely.

The headache kept me awake long enough to see the storm blowing off over the ocean. I would have appreciated the sight more if my head didn't pound in rhythm with the enormous waves. We had settled far up the shore - but I could tell this place had a high tide mark that would go above us. Must watch ...

I awoke again at dawn. The gulls still complained about

our presence. My sisters appeared to sleep, and they had an improbable amount of luggage piled up around them. I looked them over couldn't see more than a few cuts and some bruises. I hadn't noticed on the plane, being somewhat overwhelmed with their insanity, but they had dressed in a more casual style than usual. That would help because we were going to have to do some hiking before too long.

Tessa gave me a silent nod and then stared out at the waves. I wasn't sure what he searched for -- maybe just hoping for an ocean liner to come along and invite us on a nice safe cruise.

My head still pounded. That would go on for at least another day, but it had diminished to the sort of dull ache that annoyed more than hurt.

We'd been lucky to find any land, and I was happier for it than the idea of floating around in the middle of the Pacific. Not a bad looking island, I decided. Tropical. Excellent beachfront, too. The one mountain rose almost a quarter taller than a smaller one and had a slight haze of smoke, which was the sign of an active volcano. Not too active, I didn't think. There was no sign of ash or lava flows, at least where we were. Healthy trees, as well, and they'd been growing for quite a few years.

Jungle growth had spread all the way across the view, right to the edge of the sands.

Not a single sign of anyone.

That bothered me. This place was the kind of paradise that someone should have claimed. Maybe there were better beaches on the lea side, away from the oncoming storms.

Aster was the first of the sisters to wake up. She sat up

with a little yelp that woke the others.

"Oh, I had so hoped that was a nightmare," she said aloud and then looked at me. "Sunflower --"

I waved away her words before she got started. I wanted to stand up and look and around -- and have a moment of privacy -- but sitting up proved difficult. Tessa had wandered off and back since I spotted his prints in the sand. I could also see that the tide was out. I used to know the general dates and times of high and low tides in various places. Living in Omaha had sort of made that knowledge not so necessary.

I glanced back at the jungle and felt an odd shiver, though I didn't know why. I like jungles.

"Have you seen anything?" I asked Tessa.

"Nothing of note," he admitted. He winced as he looked around. "We got lucky, Summerfield. We all survived. I don't know where it will go from here, but at least the weather is better today."

I wanted to discuss Dagon and the storm, but not while the Unholy Five were with us. A couple of them wandered off to some gigantic rocks down the beach, scattering gulls again. They took turns watching for monsters, all five of them making the trek. Violet even carried a suitcase and changed into what must be her vacation clothing, including sandals. Practical, as always.

I had no other clothes, but at least what I wore felt comfortable once I shook the sand out of my shirt. I thought about ditching my shoes and socks. One of my sisters would put them in the luggage -- but right now, I didn't feel safe enough to run barefoot across the sands.

"I can't get a connection," Violet admitted, holding out

her rather fancy phone. "I had hoped --"

She stopped and looked as bothered as I had ever seen her. Violet, my oldest sister, headed the law firm and directed things. She looked at the device as though it had personally insulted her.

"We will not have that kind of luck." I didn't mention how the continued silence made me think we were alone here. I couldn't even see signs of paths in the jungle that would have led to this beach.

"At least we survived," Rose whispered, as though testing those words.

I nodded agreement, and my head did not explode. Not having cell coverage was annoying. I wanted a simple answer to get us out of here.

And when was the last time that had happened?

Birds in the jungle put up a racket that startled us all. I even got to my feet. Tessa moved a little closer to the noise but then came back with a shake of his head.

"Nothing I saw," he admitted. He shook more sand from his clothing. "We need to decide what to do for today. Rest would be wise and wait to see if anyone happens along this beach. If not, by tomorrow, we might start looking for help."

This was the first step in what was going to be trouble. My sisters were used to being in charge. Tessa always had people listen to him. I didn't want to get caught in the middle of this mess --

"Rest would be good," Rose admitted, surprising me. She'd had any contact with Tessa before now. "Just rest and see if we can figure anything else. I apologize to both of you, though. This was not our best plan."

"You can apologize over dinner back in Omaha," I said. "Let's focus on what we need to survive. And we are lucky, you know. I do have some knowledge in living off the land, particularly in jungles."

They all five looked at me as though I had just grown wings.

"Do you people ever pay attention?" I asked with a bit of humor this time. "I lived in jungles with mom and dad, both with indigenous natives in the Amazon basin and somewhat in Peru. We can survive this long enough to get rescued. I can't guarantee the vacation will be pleasant, but we'll make it."

Even Tessa appeared relieved at those words. It also, I supposed, put me in charge. That was fine. I knew what to do.

Or I would if my head stopped pounding.

I stared out at the ocean. The plane sat on its side and with one wing in the air. The other seemed to have dug into the ocean's shallow area by the island and brought us to a stop. I could even see the door still open and wondered how much water had gotten inside. The waves were not so high now, at least.

"I can swim out to the plane," I said, startling them. "If we salvage some equipment, we might get it to work before the saltwater ruins it. That has to be a priority for today. I can't guarantee either the tides or the storms after this."

"I'll swim out there with you," Carnation said. She had always been fond of swimming. "It doesn't look too bad. That's a bit of a protected bay."

I squinted. Carnation was right. The waves broke over a line of rocks that must have been not far under the water.

Better still.

"I'll go," Tessa said. "Yes, Summerfield, I can swim and quite well."

"You don't need to rush out there just yet," Lily added. She settled on the sand and leaned back on his arm. "Rest for a bit, Sunflower. You haven't even been conscious for half an hour. Waiting isn't a bad idea."

I almost argued but changed my mind because I realized that breathing hurt my head and thinking wasn't much better.

"Yeah. It's not as if the plane is going anywhere," Tessa said and leaned back as well.

And at that point, a gigantic tentacle reached out of the waves, wrapped itself around the small jet, and dragged it off into the water.

We sat in stunned silence while the ocean roiled. One massive eye came up to look our way. Then it slid away. I saw the tip of the plane for a moment as the creature dragged it across the bay.

"No, we are not going swimming," Tessa decided.

"I think," Rose began, her voice a little high. She cleared her throat. "I think maybe we should move off the beach."

No one argued. Everyone gathered up luggage and headed toward that edge of the jungle, even though it had not looked so hospitable a moment before.

I glanced back at the bay and spotted the most enormous octopus I'd ever seen as it dragged the plane over those submerged rocks, the shape clear for a moment. Then it pulled the plane down under the water, where it belched up a bit of debris and disappeared. I knew we'd never see it again.

That meant no one else would see it either.

"Well," Violet said.

We all nodded as we paused at the edge of the jungle. I was not ready for that change and even looked up at the sky in the vain hope that something might fly by. A helicopter would be nice about now -- but I couldn't say where we had crashed. That kept me from wishing for help. What if I got us a helicopter, but it didn't have enough fuel to get back off the island? What if it crashed into the bay, too, and gave Octozilla another play toy?

Maybe the octopus kept people away from this beach. How close would it come to shore? I knew some of the creatures in aquariums had developed prodigious climbing skills when going for something they wanted.

I went to the edge of the jungle with the others. It didn't look any better than the water right now. Who knew what might hide in those trees? I'd spent enough time in the jungles of Brazil to understand that this sort of ecosystem was not somewhere you headed into on a whim. We would need things. Sticks to beat off snakes would be nice. I had nothing against reptiles as long as the dangerous ones kept their distance. My sisters had their own feelings toward them.

We could find food, though. Despite the headache, my brain dragged back information I hadn't needed for quite a while.

"By now, people will know we didn't reach the resort," Lily said and looked up at the sky. Good reminder! I had forgotten we'd been heading somewhere. "I imagine they'll start looking for us, and I don't think we went that far off the lanes, either."

"No one will see the plane," Rose pointed out.

"There are rocks and branches," I said with a wave of my arm. "We can spell out 'help' about midway up the beach. Big letters, at least six feet -- you'll see those from quite a distance on white sand like that one. It should stay for a day or two, and we'll rebuild it if the tide washes the word away."

No one argued. I suspected the Unholy Five felt more than a little contrite about having dragged me here. I felt guilty about breaking Tessa's magic and about Dagon. We would get out of this, though. My people would hear that we were all missing, right? They paid attention to the news these days. Even if the Fae didn't catch on, there were others at the Fortress who would see the announcement and spread the word. They had a link to me. If the humans didn't pick us up, my Fae would.

I helped move the rocks. I had limited knowledge of the Pacific Islands, so I did not know where we were. No matter. There was nowhere on Earth that wasn't under someone's watchful eye, right?

So why hadn't the Fae found us yet?

I needed to talk to Tessa, but I never got him alone during that hot, humid day. I watched the sun. We were close to the equator.

I also dared to go a little distance into the jungle and found some coconuts and breadfruit, so we had a bit to munch on, plus the liquid to drink. That last turned out to be more fun than I had expected. Maybe we were all getting silly since we realized we had survived. That was okay. I had faith that someone would rescue us.

Any moment now.

We soon had *HELP* spelled out on the beach. I started

making a hut up near the trees -- nothing fancy, but a little cover from the breeze that had picked up, and I feared another downpour. Clouds began to rise and came closer. I even thought it was Dagon's work, and maybe that wouldn't be so bad because my people would sense that disturbance.

I watched the storm as it blew up over the ocean, a pretty thing as long as it stayed away from the island. Lighting flashed across the sky in the distance, but above that, we could see an array of stars, more and brighter than I had seen in years. The moon rose over the two peaks behind us since we faced the east.

We sat on the shore for a while. I'd done my best to make the hut rainproof, and we had the luggage in there. Tomorrow I planned on finding more food and perhaps a better place to shelter. We didn't want to go too far from our beach and hope of rescue.

I wanted to talk to Tessa, but we still were not alone. He stared out at the sky and didn't look so dismayed. Maybe he hadn't thought we could survive, being mere humans -- and him being one of us for the moment.

Tessa looked at me and sighed. "People back at the Fortress will know by now," he said. I had been thinking the same thing. "Some of them are apt to do crazy things. At least Kala is visiting her mother."

I nodded, but there was still another problem. "Brandis might react just as much."

"True," Tessa agreed. My sisters were being quiet and looking contrite, as they should under the circumstances. "That goes with being --" Tessa stopped and glanced at the storm, and I knew he was rethinking his words. "That goes with being one of the top people in security."

"He'll think he's failed," I said with a sudden new dread. "That's not good."

"No, it isn't," Tessa agreed. "But it also means he's going to be contacting everyone he knows. If anyone can track us down, I have faith in Brandis to do so. I just don't think it'll be easy."

"We're sorry," Carnation said aloud, and the other four nodded miserably. "This wasn't our wisest move."

I could have said a few things. Instead, I held back my frustration toward them and myself.

"You couldn't have expected anything like the storm," I admitted. "But even so, this whole idea was over the top for you to try."

"You've just been so overworked," Lily replied with a wave of her hands. "You were doing odd things, SB, and need a rest."

"Next time, let me pick the vacation spot."

They were still apologetic but also adamant about my behavior. I came close to telling my sisters about the Fae and magic --

But then looked at Tessa and realized that I couldn't prove any of it right now. There was one other aspect about this disaster in my favor, though. This was going to give me power over my sisters for years.

All we had to do was survive.

CHAPTER 7

The next morning, I awoke to find Violet leaning over me and nudging my shoulder. I did not want to wake up because I knew this would not be a better day. I already felt hot, uncomfortable, and sandy.

"Come on, Sunflower," Violet insisted. "We need you."

I pushed up on an elbow, still half asleep and fighting to remain that way. "Call me Sunflower one more time, and I'll send my friend the dragon to have a few words with you."

Not the thing to say to Violet. I came awake as I looked at her startled and then worried face. Oh yes, an excellent way to remind them that they already thought I'm crazy.

I laughed. "Well, that was an odd dream! Pretty sure we have no dragons here. What is wrong?"

"Food," Violet said. She sounded rather plaintive, too.

Fishing in the bay was right out. Would there be any freshwater fish somewhere?

I'd been the last to crawl into the hut and sleep, having taken an extended watch for planes. Now I came out and stretched, took off my shirt, shook out the sand and a few bugs, and looked around. Yeah, this was still a deserted beach. No sign of anyone but my companions.

The elation of having survived had given way to other emotions. I saw annoyance in Rose but worry in Lily and

Carnation. Violet and Aster appeared determined. Those two could keep the others going.

"I hope Tom and the kids aren't too worried," Carnation mumbled, looking out at the ocean.

I put a hand on her arm and realized I hadn't considered their families -- or our grandparents. Chances were that our parents wouldn't know about this until well after the adventure. My people would also worry, though. I hope that paid off.

"Okay." The tide had not come up too high to wash away our help sign. "This is a good time to watch for planes. Tessa and I can go find food."

Aster looked like she would argue about the two of us hunting. Then she glanced at the jungle and changed her mind. I thought Tessa might want to discuss going into the wilderness. If he could go cat, he would have been happier. I wanted to apologize again, but it wouldn't help.

I stayed long enough to help the Unholy Five set up some makeup mirrors to flash at the sky and promised we'd be back by noon. That gave me a few hours to scout out this area of the island and talk with Tessa about things I did not want my sisters to hear. It might even involve dragons.

The five stayed on the beach while Tessa and I hiked into the jungle. I thought Violet wanted one of them to go with us, but I saw Aster talking with her and shaking her head. That might have to do with trust.

"Watch out for snakes," I said as we headed into the trees.

Tessa mumbled something indistinct. I didn't ask. The jungle growth took all our attention for the first half-hour, but then we came to a glade of sorts with scattered plants. We paused there at the edge and watched as birds swept in at the bugs. Some type of small mammal -- probably a guinea pig -- dashed off into the trees when I moved.

"We can rest," I said with a wave toward a fallen tree. "Just watch out --"

"Yeah," Tessa replied. He walked around the moss-covered trunk, pounded it a few times, and even lifted one end and let it drop again. A small, startled lizard ran for his life.

We sat down.

"How are you feeling?" he asked after a moment's silence.

"My head is still off. I threatened Violet with a visit from a dragon if she didn't stop calling me Sunflower. I passed it off as a nightmare, and it is one, just not what she thinks."

"They have no right to judge your sanity, not after what they did."

"I won't argue," I said with a laugh. "And my sisters know they went too far, even without the crash. I may have some peace for a while if we can get out of this mess. Living the rest of my life on this island with my sisters and a disgruntled Cat Totem does not appeal to me."

"We'll figure it out," he said and watched where some beautiful hyacinth parrots flew across the opening. "I haven't come up with a way to break the oath -- at least nothing that doesn't include one of us dying. Since I have the magic, you'd have to be the person to die. I don't think that would work. Confronting death is an end of a journey."

"Not the answer I'm looking for," I admitted. "At the moment, my sisters are contrite and cooperating, but that won't last."

"They aren't stupid. They'll do whatever it takes to stay

alive here."

I nodded and went out into this wild field, surprised because I had spotted some potatoes, corn, and even peppers. I found squash growing up some trees at the edge of the opening, and between the two of us, we managed quite a haul, tying everything up in our shirts. No, we would not starve, though I imagined this fare might get old fast. Still, I knew how to cook such things. The gourds were an excellent find if we found a fresh water source.

Or if it rained again -- and I suspected the weather would soon change for the worst. The tall trees obscured the sky.

"A lot of birds here," I said. "Some of them aren't long-distance flyers, either. But they must have brought the seeds that have grown these plants -- they're native to the west coast of South America. So maybe -- maybe we're closer to the continent than we think."

"I would like that," Tessa admitted. "That could mean someone will come by before too long."

"That's my hope." And yet I had seen no signs -- ah, but we hadn't explored far. "We might have to hike to the other side and see what's there, too. Up the mountain, not along the shore. I don't trust Octozilla to keep his distance."

Tessa laughed at that one, but he agreed. We studied the landscape and the plant life. Some of it had taken advantage of flooded areas and places where the volcanic stone might be too close to the surface to support taller growth. I did not see any sign of new lava beds, though. That was a plus.

We had started back to the others, but I still had a couple questions.

"Why can't the fae find us? They have some link on me,"

I said with a frown.

"It is an enormous world to check. We don't know where our friends might look, or if anyone outside of your sisters knew they were heading out over the Pacific -- at least not until word gets out that we didn't show up at this paradise they'd planned."

"But they will track us down."

"Eventually," he said and then frowned. "I can sense some magic around us, though."

"I thought so, too."

"I suspect it is the remnant of Dagon's storm, and it might block any sign of either of us -- if they even considered looking for me without my powers attached. We have messed that up, too."

"Let's try not to let the others realize how stupid we've been," I suggested.

"They drugged us, Summerfield. I'm holding that as the real excuse we have for our part in this mess."

"I suspect they will still give us trouble."

"Much as you are going to annoy your sisters over this."

"Karma," I said.

"What is that sound?"

I could hear it now that he asked, an odd loud screeching noise, but I didn't recognize a bird that made that sound --

Not birds. We found a colony of capuchins who vociferously argued with some mustached tamarins who had wandered into their vicinity.

I watched, surprised. "The birds didn't bring those guys here," I said. Then I had a little hope. "Maybe this is a conservation zone. That could mean someone is watching from somewhere on the island."

"Who missed our spectacular arrival?" Tessa asked.

"They might be on the other side of the mountains, out of the storm path."

Tessa nodded. I didn't think he had much hope for such a simple answer. However, the primates decided to swim across the ocean to reach here.

But a look at the sky unsettled me again.

"Clouds coming in," I said. "We had better get back. We have enough food for today."

He looked up and nodded. The tamarins had backed off from the battle, and we left a place of peace behind. I wanted ... I don't know what. Maybe that we had a peaceful little paradise, a nice vacation despite such an odd start.

"We won't have to worry about food," I said, shifting the weight of my shirt on my shoulder. "Everything is plentiful. We are almost on the equator, so we won't get cold, except in the storms. The rain means we'll have fresh water, too."

"Not as bad as it could have been," Tessa agreed. "After all, we might have been Octozilla snacks."

"True. This way. I want a look at the edge of the closer hills."

Tessa didn't argue. I wondered if he had ever been outside of civilization, but I didn't ask. I tried not to consider how many years Tessa had lived. He fit into my life too well.

The wind picked up.

"Dagon, I think."

"Yes," Tessa agreed. He looked up. "That might not be so bad. The others know Dagon remains fixated on you. It might help them track us down."

A good side to it.

"I wish --"

Tessa clamped a hand on my arm. "Don't."

I had already stopped those words. Even going that far had spiked the headache. I hoped the pain backed down again. That had been blood pressure, I thought.

"Damn. I need better control."

"We are managing fine now that we've survived. You did that much, Summerfield. We can handle the rest. Hold on to that wish for a time when we're in real danger again, and then word it just as well as you did for the crash."

"Yes," I said and forced myself to keep walking. "I realized at the last moment that if I wished for the plane to survive, that didn't mean that we would."

"Yeah. So, you focused on the people and let the plane go. It was the best choice, but harder to wish for living things than for planes. If you have to do it again, I'll do my best to watch over you afterward. However, it would be better if you don't have to. It's dangerous for you. That's not how I want my powers back. Besides, you are the one who knows how to survive here."

"I think --" I looked around again, and it occurred to me that I had a fantastic opportunity here. "I think I can approach this as a study, Tessa. A class project. This is an unusual island. I have nothing to write on, but I am good at making mental notes."

This put me in a curiously cheerful mood. I found myself amused because, when it came down to it, this would have been my favorite kind of vacation, anyway. Here I was exploring somewhere new and making links to other places.

"We have seen no large land-dwelling mammals," I pointed out. "But there are some small ones, plus the primates and birds -- and everything I've spotted so far has been indigenous to the west coast and Amazon basin of South America. This is not where I would have expected to find such a collection of them."

"I am not at all surprised that we've stumbled on something odd," Tessa agreed. "I spent most of my time in the human world in Europe and North America. This is out of my realm of understanding."

"It's curious," I said and looked around again. "I wonder what else we're going to find here."

CHAPTER 8

The storm blew up sooner than I had expected, and I was glad we were already heading back to the others. We took a different path that wound close to the hillside, out of the wind, and I spotted a good-sized overhang along the edge of an ancient lava flow. That would be a better cover in this weather. We left the food supplies there and made a faster trip to the beach.

However, getting my sisters to head into the jungle, even in the face of the oncoming storm, proved more difficult than I had expected. They'd been cooperative until now.

"We need to go," I said with some exasperation as they dawdled and suggested tomorrow might be better. "This is not safe, Flowers!" I had not used that term since I was five, but they drove me to that reaction. "The wind is dangerous enough --" Tessa grabbed luggage from the covering that would not hold up to this much weather and jogged for the tree line.

Lightning struck the beach so close that we all felt the tingle.

"Go! Dangerous!"

Yes, that got them moving at last. We rushed into the jungle, which wasn't safe in this wind either, never mind the lightning.

"Not seen any snakes," I shouted when I saw Carnation looking up in the trees with open dread. The others heard and looked with startled stares all around -- but they followed Tessa, and I kept to the rear of the line so that we didn't lose any of them.

It occurred to me that my sisters had never seen me working out in the field. I suppose I had a few things to prove, and we impressed them when we led them to the overhang, which protected us from rain, falling branches, and the wind.

A couple marmosets had taken up residence and had raided a bit of the food, but not enough to matter. They took off into the storm, and I wished them luck. The others had settled against the wall and looked happier to be inside something more tangible than a few poles and big leaves.

"Lava Cave," I said, pointing back toward the end I had not yet explored. "It is a tube made when the rock cools enough to form over the top of a lava flow. Ancient, so don't worry. I've seen nothing active here except maybe some steam vents on the higher mountain, not this one. When the storm passes, I'll find what we need to cook the food. We have some aguaymanto -- I think you'll like them."

I passed around some small orange and yellow fruit, parsing them out to all of us. They tasted sweet and tart and proved a delightful treat while the rain poured down. We rested.

Maybe I could find some area to fish tomorrow. I would not suggest guinea pig.

"We won't have any trouble holding on here," I said. "We might move higher up the mountain and try bonfires if we have to -- but since this is a volcanic landmass, that might not draw any attention. However, it will give us a better view. The island is odd. I think this could be a government wildlife reserve."

That cheered them up. I wasn't sure why. But I talked about what I'd seen and --

And I stopped. I'd been looking at Lily, but my eyes focused on the wall just beyond her, though it remained all but invisible in the dull light of the stormy day.

I moved closer. Lily might have thought I saw something dangerous from the way she froze -- but no. My hand reached out and brushed against the surface of the wall.

Carvings.

Lily brought out her phone and let the light show what I'd found. I couldn't speak for a moment.

"Old," I said. "There is almost something Incan in the look -- that's possible. Oh, and there --"

I saw the rim of a bowl with a chipped edge peeking out of a pile of leaves. There were several other pieces, most of them intact. I didn't touch them. Sacrilege to take even this one, but we could use it to cook in and gather water.

"This is Incan," I said, holding it up. "Late Inca, in fact. Nice designs. You can shut down the light. We might need it later."

Lily did. I took the find to the front of the overhang and used the rainwater to wash it out. My mind was working far too fast now. Once clean, I gathered water and sipped, and then passed the bowl to the others, even though I hated to let it out of my hands.

"It is possible," I began and then stopped, running

through the hypothesis again. I couldn't know, but at least it would make an entertaining tale. "It might be possible that a group of people left from the Peruvian coast in small craft and headed here. Pizzaro's men intercepted one such raft filled with gold and silver. It could not have been a big migration, but they could have brought food, plants, and even animals."

"And stumbled onto this shelter," Rose said, looking around. "No one ever found them."

"They might have died out too soon. Those carvings are far cruder than the pottery, but I bet the person who used this pottery made them. It's possible the people brought Smallpox with them and didn't survive for that reason. It was wiping out most of the Inca, even killing the Sapa Inca, about the time Pizzaro arrived."

"Sapa Inca?" Tessa asked.

"The great Inca ruler. The Inca Empire was in the middle of a civil war over who should take the throne. Before the Inca could settle the question, the Spanish destroyed the country."

"Yes, I remember," Tessa said and then looked at me, smiling. "I recall reading about what happened there."

Ha. Tessa had been alive when the Spanish invaded, though he would not have been part of the army, being fae and not interested in human wars.

"It had to be more than one raft," I added, looking back out at the world beyond our little covering. "I don't remember seeing anything related to such a migration, but it's probable that a few people leaving went unrecorded in that time of trouble."

"They Kon-Tiki'd it to get here?" Aster asked. She

sounded fascinated.

"That would be my guess." I gathered more water and passed it around again. "Although, I can't imagine it all happened at once. I saw not only coastal food out there but also Amazonian Basin animals. That might mean more than one migration."

"That's amazing," Rose admitted. "How can you get so much information from a carving and a bowl?"

"I recognize the style of the work," I said, looking at the red, black, and yellowish geometric design. After a longer drink, I filled it again and passed the ancient bowl around once more. "The rest is a guess based on some odd array of plants and animals I saw out there. The food we collected are all plants that the Inca grew, and they are not the pre-cultivation wild versions."

They all looked surprised. I didn't think it was the knowledge. Maybe it was just how excited I sounded about it.

"Hey, this is the work I both trained for and lived in," I reminded them. "I can tell that this was an early campsite by someone who might have come here from the bay, just like us. They didn't live in here long, but since they left the pottery, I bet they died somewhere else and never made it back. The plants, birds, and primates survived, though quite a few of those species likely became locally extinct as well."

I looked toward the opening, wishing (silently) that the storm would go away. I wanted to hunt for other signs.

The weather grew more frantic, and I knew I would not get out for the rest of the day. We did map out a spot nearby and downhill for privacy. No one went there alone. We ate more fruit instead. We'd have to wait until tomorrow to make a fire to roast potatoes, squash, and the rest.

Could I find more treasures in the cave? There wasn't enough light to explore. I fought aside the frustration at being held back when I'd found something worth doing here. I tried not to act sullen. My head hurt still, but I thought another night of rest would clear that up and maybe make it a little easier to study this ... well, this fascinating island.

I told them more Inca stories. Some of them were not pleasant, but my sisters were not squeamish, anyway. They liked to learn things. We had that much in common, though they thought my constant return to college for new subjects might have been excessive.

They didn't say so tonight.

"You want to know what is amusing?" I asked as we settled in to use suitcases for pillows. "This is turning into a perfect vacation for me."

"That's not funny," Violet replied in her best 'I am the eldest' voice.

"Maybe not to you. I'm amused because I have warned you about Karma, right?"

Aster laughed.

The sun went down -- and that was when three capuchins scrambled in out of the rain and stopped in shock, finding their refuge already occupied. They settled, though, and seemed not to mind so much.

"What should we do?" Tessa asked.

"Leave them there," I said. "They make good guards, and we can all get some sleep."

My sisters either trusted me or were too tired to care. Tessa watched the monkeys until the group formed up into a fuzzy little ball and slept. Then he turned to me, knowing I was still awake but said nothing. Then Tessa went to sleep as well. He twitched at every sound. We were all lucky that he couldn't go cat just out of instinct.

I remained aware of all the sounds as well and napped rather than slept. None of my sisters rested with any comfort. I tried to feel sorry for them, but I had bruises on bruises, too. We were all stiff and sore, and while I had something fun to study tomorrow, they worried about their families.

I fretted about my clan. I had to believe that we would all get out of this. My people would not allow any other answer.

Dawn came with a fall of rain, but not as bad as the night before. Birds yelled somewhere not far away, and our little guards began playing in the miniature waterfall. They even dared come in and beg for food when we started passing around the last of the fruit.

"They might think we're just overgrown, hairless cousins," Carnation suggested. She delighted in giving them treats. Since I knew there was plenty of food not far beyond our cave, I thought it a pleasant pastime for the others.

I waited for the rain to pass and used the time to study the carvings again. They were a few crude marks of Inca symbols I'd seen often enough that I didn't mistake them. I wished there were more because I couldn't decide the context from so few. Perhaps the last inhabitant had been uneducated and only scratched in designs he remembered seeing. The cave went back a few more yards, but I saw nothing at all on those walls.

I studied the pottery, too, but without digging it up so others could observe in context when someone came to explore this place. I might have taken enough anthropology and archeology classes of late to make sure I was part of the team.

When the rain ended, we emptied one piece of luggage, and Tessa, Lily, and I went out to find food. We were all so stiff and sore from sleeping on a rock, and the others didn't even make a token offer of going with us. I didn't blame them. If I hadn't been so excited about finding something, I would have crawled into a corner of the cave and slept through the day.

I considered suggesting Lily stay behind but then remembered how the person who had last lived in that flimsy protection had never come back. I decided it was necessary if Lily and Tessa both could recognize edible plants.

Lily seemed intrigued by what I showed her. We left her digging up a few potatoes while Tessa and I tried for some more coconuts. As soon as I found a good tree, I climbed up -- Tessa didn't like that much -- and dropped coconuts down to him and then slid back down. I had not done that since my teens. Good to know that some skills stayed with a person.

"I am finding all of this frustrating, Summerfield," he said as we packed up our finds.

"You are having the ultimate lesson in being human."

"That is not amusing -- but I suppose it is true." He mumbled something again. I didn't ask, though it was not in English.

Lily had a nice gathering of potatoes, and she'd found some more peppers nearby as well.

"I need a garden when I get back home," she decided.

"You live in a High-Rise, Lily," I reminded her.

"I'd put it on the roof. People do that in New York, don't they?"

"The building owner might protest -- oh, you own it, don't you?"

"Yes. I bought the others out after you bought yours. Unlike you, though, I don't give the apartments away."

"My people work for them," I said and smiled at Tessa just in case he took this the wrong way --

And Tessa hit a loose rock and went down with a yelp of pain. By the time I knelt but had grabbed hold of his ankle and muttered very many things, which made me glad he didn't have magic right then.

"Oh hell," Lily whispered, near to panic. "Are you alright?"

"I think he has sprained or broken his ankle." I looked it over without touching it, but I could already see the swelling. "We need to get him back to the cave. Tessa --"

"Yes, yes." He looked at his ankle with a stare that said it had personally offended him. "This is not amusing."

"No, it isn't," I agreed. I did not mention how it made Tessa more human, either. It was, in fact, a real problem for the two of us. I wouldn't be able to talk alone to Tessa for a while about what we could do to attract the others.

"I could wish," I started, but Tessa put a hand on my arm and shook his head. "Let's just get him back."

It was not an easy walk for Tessa. I didn't want a break, which would be dangerous for him.

Someone would find us soon, though one thing had begun to worry me. I had not heard a boat or a plane all day and hadn't seen contrails in the sky, either -- those harbingers of the modern world that showed almost everywhere in the world these days.

No signs of any technology.

I was getting a very odd feeling about our little island paradise.

CHAPTER 9

Tessa was all but white and faint by the time we got back to the others. Aster took over caring for him. She might have been the head of hospital administration -- and the CEO -- but she had learned a few things while there. I just sat by the front of the cave and tried to calm again.

"Sprained. We've got enough cloth to make a good brace, but you must stay off your foot for a while, Tessa," she said.

That was better news than I had feared. If Tessa had broken his ankle, I would have used a wish to help him. That would have caused considerable trouble, but I didn't want Tessa down and helpless.

Since the rain had stopped for the moment, I took the bowl and went out to make us some cooked potatoes with some peppers for some spice. I started to think I'd have to climb up the volcano for some fire, but the bit of dry tinder from the cave finally crackled, and I could see a thin thread of smoke. My hands were sore from rubbing the sticks together, but I was glad for the results.

It took a few hours, of course. The others slept or mumbled, but by the time the evening storms blew in, we had an enjoyable meal. It helped.

"This improves things," Tessa admitted. He sat with his

injured ankle out in front of him, and we were careful to avoid hitting him.

"You seem sane, Tessa," Rose said, which won a laugh from both Tessa and me. "No, I mean it. I feel you have no limit in opportunities. So why are you working for Sunflower?"

"With me," I corrected. "And are you suggesting I'm not sane?"

"I'm still trying to decide," Rose said, and I suspected she might mean those words. "But you, Dion Tessa -- yes, I know your full name -- what are you doing with Sunflower?"

"You know I used to read Tarot cards for a living. You think this is less sane?" Tessa asked.

"I'm not sure."

"We run an organization that is reclaiming land for wildlife, Rose," I said.

"Oh, that, yes. Doing well, too -- but what about the rest of it?"

I was about to say something, but Tessa spoke before I could.

"Working with Summerfield means you don't get bored," Tessa explained and even managed a smile. "That's important to me. Besides, look at all the other perks. We live in the Fortress, which isn't anything to complain about -- well, as long as the FBI or drug lords aren't after us. We are also reporters for an internationally famous -- or is that infamous? -- newspaper. As crazy as that sounds, it is an intriguing job. And then, of course, there are these unexpected vacations."

I laughed. Tessa acted more himself, but they didn't realize it. I thought he felt more at ease with the Unholy Five, which helped.

I had to believe there would be an end to this vacation.

Before the next storm rushed over us, Aster and I went down to the beach and checked our Help sign. It was still there, and the waves had washed up around it. I reinforced a couple spots while Aster watched for Octozilla. She spotted him far out once, and we headed back into the jungle.

We ate fruit and nuts this time. Great diet, I thought, if any of us had needed to lose weight. It might help Rose with her blood pressure, though. Maybe I could recommend it to others.

The storm came rose in billowing clouds in the late afternoon. We had this down now, and we remained snug in our cave. The capuchins came and brought a couple more friends. However, they lingered at the front of the opening, sometimes making disparaging sounds when the wind blew their way.

Tessa told stories that night. He kept magic out of them, but I could tell before too long that he related tales about his own life. He had a knack with words and an ability to make things both fascinating and humorous so that the Unholy Five laughed as much as I did.

It was an excellent way to spend the afternoon as the storm roared outside. The poor capuchins came in out of the wet area and nestled close to us. Not even Violet, who had no use for pets, seemed upset to have one snuggle in by her side. Tessa told quieter tales then, and if I hadn't known better, I would have thought he was using magic.

The storm had been as powerful as the others, and the winds might have been worse. I heard branches falling.

However, it was dying down before the sun had set. Maybe even Dagon could not keep up this kind of assault.

Good and bad. The more the Assyrian god worked up the storms, the more likely someone from my group would notice. I was growing desperate for my clan to arrive. Oh, but I didn't want them to rush without thought of what they might find. They couldn't just pop up, could they? They'd know I was with my sisters. Maybe they were working on a safer way for people to get to us.

Maybe, maybe. I still considered telling the five about the fae, but Tessa was no closer to having his powers back, and I didn't want to die to prove a point. It was best to leave things as they were for now.

The storm blew over. We still had some daylight.

"I'm going to pick up some fallen fruit," I said as I crawled toward the opening. "We might as well take advantage of the windfall."

"I'll go with you," Lily said and followed. "I need a bathroom break, anyway."

We went out, and I found stuff not far away while Lily found a secluded spot. I'd have to bring the others out, one at a time -- or trust them to go in pairs. And Tessa --

Lily appeared at the side of a tree and frantically signaled me to come to her. When I started to speak, she shook her head. I didn't like it.

I didn't like what she showed me even more.

Footprints in the mud. Human prints, no shoes, and heading inland. They couldn't have been more than a few minutes old. I looked around with shock and worry. We had been loud and not tried to hide our own passages through the jungle.

And we were not alone.

"Back to the cave," I whispered. "We have to move out of this area."

Lily didn't argue.

I kept the suitcase packed with fruits and nuts. We might need the food if we had to hide and didn't dare go scavenging. Tessa knew there was something wrong the moment we arrived back at the cave. Rose realized it as well.

"Grab everything you can and get ready to go," I said. Lily was already working at packing away clothing and carefully packed our bowl. "We found prints -- there are other humans here, and I suspect they're natives since they weren't wearing any shoes. My thought is to leave most of the stuff and take what we'll need for a few days. The footprints came from the direction of the bay, so he'll have seen the message we left that message on the sand."

"You think he's dangerous," Rose said. She'd grabbed a shoulder bag and shoved a few things inside.

"I can't be certain, but I've had contact with enough indigenous tribes to know it's best to be careful. We only saw a sign of one, but I'm betting on far more."

"Where are we going to go?" Violet asked. No argument, at least.

"Up to the highest point of this mountain," I said, glancing outside and hoping we had time to away -- though I wasn't sure we would be any safer. "I want us up high enough to get a better look at the island. Hey, what would a wilderness vacation be without a hike?"

None of my sisters seemed amused. Tessa looked

downright worried, his hand going to his leg.

"I'll find something you can use as a cane, Tessa," I said. Aster gave a quick nod.

I went out and located a sturdy fallen branch from nearby. I'd find something better along the way if we needed to, but my spidey sense said to get clear right now.

Close to the cave, we found another set of footprints. This might have been the same person, and he was still alone. Good.

"We'll follow," I whispered. "As long as our visitor remains ahead of us, we'll be safer. Tessa? Can you do this?"

Tessa leaned on the cane, and Aster helped him walk. He gave a silent nod.

I wasn't sure how far we would go today. We soon climbed out of the jungle itself, and that meant we had more light --

And the footprints lead to a stone-lined walkway that wound upward toward the peak.

"Well, damn," I said and stopped again. There was, in fact, a bench by the path. Tessa sat down there. I settled on the ground, too shaken to keep moving. My sisters just stared. "Damn. More than one person. Many more for a building project like this one. Inca people built extensive roads from about Quito in Ecuador down to Santiago in Chile along the Pacific shore and another on the other side of the mountains, with many connecting roads. The style is much the same but on a smaller scale."

"What do we do?" Rose asked. She looked up the path, but there was just enough growth in the way that we couldn't see anything except dark plants and the lighter stonework as it zig-zagged back and forth up the hillside. I could see the pattern of it now and perhaps the movement of the man we followed, a shadow jogging upward. News of strangers on the island would soon reach ... someone.

"We should wait a little longer. I think we can take this in the moonlight. No sign of storms. We might want to scout for ourselves before anyone comes along to take us in. Tessa - _"

"Up," he said with a nod. "Since they have a bench here, I am going to believe there are others on the way up there. I'll make it."

We waited there a little longer, nibbling on food while we could. I debated with myself about whether or not we should climb up. Maybe we could still wait for my people to come and rescue us.

"Here is the one problem," I said at last as I stood. We started moving in that very last bit of sunlight. The moon would be full tonight, at least. "And it's a big and odd problem. I have never heard of an island like this in any of my studies. It would have drawn notice. I don't know how it has stayed hidden so long, but we seem to be far off the edge of any map."

I looked at Tessa. He knew the other reason I thought no one had found the island in the past. We had both sensed magic from Dagon's storms, but I feared we had found another source.

I had seen no overt signs of magic so far, but without Tessa's powers, maybe we wouldn't notice?

Damn and damn.

We started upward on an easy climb. I saw quite a few

side trails, too, most of them made of packed dirt and disappearing into wilder areas. I marked each one and pointed out the ones where we could hide.

The trail curved up and around the mountainside, and we were soon in areas we could not spot from the beach where we'd landed.

And here -- oh yes, here we saw more signs of civilization.

"Terraced planting fields." I waved at one such shadowed area where a dozen such plots, filled with potato plants, rose along the edge of a hill. That had been the staple food of the Andean cultures for a long time.

"This is more than a few people," I said. "I thought so when we found the trail, but this -- it takes a large population to maintain terraces like this. And I suspect these are just the outliers."

"Civilized, though, right?" Carnation asked. She helped Tessa now, with Aster close by.

"Yes, in their own way." I had already mentioned sacrifices. I didn't think this was the time to bring them up again.

Around the next curve, we found a small, dark building to the side of the path. I would have expected someone there, but the place proved empty.

"Tambo," I said with a wave toward the building. "Typical for Inca lands. Rest stops. We might as well take advantage of it and decide which way to go at dawn. It's apparent we're heading into something far more complex than I would have guessed."

"But you want to see," Aster said.

"Of course. That doesn't mean it's a sane idea. And isn't

that what this whole point of this holiday?"

"Huh," Violet said, too exhausted for more of an answer.

The inside was more wondrous than I had expected. Murals showed on all the walls. I just stared until the others pushed me out of the way. They were already finding spots to rest before I even noticed them again.

"You look strange, Sunflower," Aster said. She sounded worried.

"Odd," I said with a wave toward one mural illuminated by the moonlight through a window. "Very odd. I can't tell if this is Incan or Aztec -- or a hybrid combination of several cultures. Hell. It's late. Very late. Those are conquistadors carrying off people and loot to a Spanish Galleon."

That drew Rose's attention. She went closer and then looked back at me with a nod. "Well, this just gets odder by the moment, doesn't it?"

"Quetzalcoatl," I said. I brushed my hand over part of that mural, shaking my head in disbelief. "Not Incan. Aztec or perhaps even late Mayan -- but the rest of this is Inca work. Look -- it's like the Spanish are carrying the statue of the Winged Serpent to their ship."

"Along with other things," Aster pointed out. "People. Cages."

"And here," Rose added. "Tell me that isn't the same galleon being attacked by another huge octopus."

I went over to her mural. It was dark, but my eyes had adjusted, and I could see that she was right. Octozilla.

I sat down. No one bothered me.

The idea that they'd come to this island by rafts had seemed possible. The cave had been a shelter for a single person. He or she might have been someone who broke off from the larger group and lived alone.

The Spanish had been collecting treasures, people, plants, and animals to take back to Spain? Yes, I could see such a group with enough survivors to populate the island. I could even believe in a colony of giant octopi staying close to this unusual island. Or maybe it was still the same one? There was a shark up by Greenland that was somewhere over 500 years old.

No one said anything. We just waited.

Near dawn, a group went by, heading down the hill. We'd had enough warning to hide behind the outer walls, but they didn't go into the tambo. They were people heading out to work the fields, and if we didn't move on, they could spot us.

Up another switchback, and we hit an area with scraggly trees and more volcanic rock. This lava flow made it harder to farm the coarse ground, but I welcomed it as a better place to hide today.

"I could understand a few words of what the farmers were saying," I admitted when we'd settled behind some trees. Tessa moved better after a few hours of rest, but I knew we didn't want to press too hard for his sake. "I think they were speaking an ancient form of Quechua. That's spoken in parts of Peru and a few other areas."

"How can they have gone unnoticed for so long?" Violet asked. "This just doesn't seem natural."

Oh, I didn't want the conversation going in that direction.

"We're off of any regular flight paths," I said with a wave toward the spots of blue sky hidden by the trees. "I haven't even seen a contrail."

They all looked up and then back at me with nods that did not show an improvement in their moods.

"And there are the storms," Aster added. "This has to be one of the most active areas in the world."

"We are outsiders," I said with a brush at my shirt. "And no way we could fit in, even if we found some local clothing. I'm not sure how long they are going to take to find us -- but they will. They know we're around somewhere. We might break up, and some go --"

"No," Rose and Tessa chorused. Rose nodded to Tessa to continue.

"We need to stick with you as much as possible, Summerfield," he said. He sounded more serious than I was used to hearing. "You have a better chance of knowing what to expect from them."

I began dredging my memory for every bit of knowledge I had from school and my odd life.

I couldn't point out one other fact that occurred to me. The Spanish had filled the ship with treasure and slaves from more than one culture, mostly Aztech and Incan from the looks of things, although perhaps a few others like the nearby Tlaxcalans. I didn't see any other sign of contact --or if there had been others washed up on this shore, no one got back out.

This was not a hopeful thought.

CHAPTER 10

I did not know what to do now. We sat in our little spot and kept silent at the slightest sound that might be someone nearby. How long could we remain hidden? On the good side, food remained plentiful, and this being a tropical island, I didn't fear cold weather. On the unpleasant side, this was not an immense landmass, and I suspected the authorities had a large population they could find us.

"Sunflower, I'm sorry --" Aster began in one of those times when we were alone.

I lifted my hand. "Hold that thought until we are back home. We need to work this out. Any thoughts?"

Not even Tessa had anything to say this time. Then he gave a startled look toward the trail --

People headed our way, silent, and intent on the ground -- tracking us. I stood, signaled the rest of my companions to be still as I moved off to the left. I hoped to draw their attention just long enough --

My ploy didn't work. The men caught me --- Aztec from the design of their clothing and possibly even Eagle Warriors. This was not a group I wanted to annoy. They spoke, and I knew we needed to understand what they were saying.

Only one answer to that problem.

"I wish I could understand and speak your language."

Maybe they thought I tripped over a rock when I fell. They dragged me to my feet and kept me there. I understood what they said, but the words and my headache fought each other in my brain. The ten warriors, armed with spears, headed for our hiding place. I decided to stop any sort of trouble before they reached there.

"You should all come out," I said aloud. I then spoke in their language, each word causing a pain like a nail hammered into my head. "I have asked my companions to join us. Please be patient."

My ability to speak their words surprised and unsettled the men, but they seemed happy when Tessa and the Flowers showed themselves. Aster helped Tessa, who looked at me with a shake of his head. He knew what I'd done.

"We will give no trouble," Tessa said, also in the right language.

Oh, of course. Fae had an innate ability to understand words, which was not part of his magic, though tied to it. Words created magic, so knowing what others were saying helped avoid trouble. I suspected it had become a part of a camouflage instinct as well. Fae dropping into strange places would not always want to show their magic right away.

Or they might have lost the ability to use magic if they did something really, really stupid.

My sisters looked from him to me and back again with a touch of disbelief.

The warriors led us back to the trail. Tessa moved to walk by me, still using the cane. I silently cursed our lack of magic again.

I should have expected something like this, though. Oh, I know it sounds strange -- and paranoid -- but ever since I fell in with the fae, odd things continually happened to me. Very odd things. Ancient Assyrian Gods and drug lords thinking I was moving in on their territory seemed commonplace these days, so why not a lost civilization?

Brandis would take care of those troubles back at The Fortress. Even my grandparents would step in if they needed help with anything in the human world. My friends were not without friends. Officer Lenz. Agent Krieg. By now, all of them would realize that six Summerfields and one Dion Tessa had disappeared. I imagined it was crazy back there.

Don't worry, guys. We're alive.

Vane. That might be a problem. Our teenage shape-shifting dragon wasn't used to strong emotions, and I worried about him. Brandis had the best chance of keeping the boy in hand and not letting him loose in Omaha, where he could cause a panic none of us wanted to see.

Out of my hands for the moment. I could feel the brush of someone's magic as we neared the top of the hill and glanced Tessa's way to see his slight nod. I did not imagine it. We were heading to a place with considerable power.

The path led around a volcanic outcropping that looked like it might be almost pure obsidian. I could see where workers had chipped flakes away -- and yes, the spears had obsidian tips. Lethal, those things. Worse than regular blades --

We continued forward around the outcrop. Violet made a sound of surprise.

I looked away from the obsidian to find an immense city

cascading down the hillside. Not a village -- a *city* with stone buildings, wide roads, and in the distance a harbor. Small fishing boats were out in the bay. I saw a town square with statues, though I couldn't make them out at this distance. To the left I found a large ball court. Just to our right sat a stepped pyramid that rose several levels above us. It had remained hidden behind the peak of the mountain we had been climbing. The curve of the hills had even muffled the sounds of the townspeople.

The higher active volcano stood above it all, still showing a thin edge of steam.

I looked back to the town. Ten thousand? Twenty? Terraced fields stretched out on both sides, making an enormous bowl -- this must have been the caldera of an even older volcano.

Well, damn. Despite the pounding in my head, I felt a wave of awe.

This was a cultural anthropologist's heaven. Unfortunately, the warriors were in a hurry to take us down to the city. I wanted to go straight to the temple, but it might have some bad connotations for strangers in this society. I couldn't do more than glance at the building as we went past the lower level. Was that a stone for sacrifice part way up?

Study something else.

Tessa kept twitching in that direction, though. I realized it was the source of the magic, and I could almost sense it radiating outward in a wall. There might be a reason no one had found this place. A shield of some sort?

Fae magic?

No. I knew the feel of fae powers, and this came from

something different. I could perceive that in the touch of it, which seemed to permeate the entire city.

As we moved down from the temple level, we found groups of inhabitants. People looked at us as we passed. I saw open curiosity, but no panic and no actual surprise. That told me something more. They had seen outsiders before.

However, those strangers had contributed nothing noticeable to this society. Clothing still mimicked ancient cotton and wool patterns, but they had worked those designs into a coarser woven cloth. No cotton plants, and no llamas or alpacas, then. Weapons kept the pre-Spanish style, but that might have been a purposeful dismissal of anything Spanish that came off the ship with them.

Oh, how I wished this were a better circumstance, and I could study without any worries. Well, we needed research anyway, I supposed. The more we learned, the fewer mistakes we would make.

Messengers came to talk to our guards. I heard a guard say that we understood, and that drew attention. The messenger moved away with one man. The conversation did not take long, and I couldn't hear it.

We were moving again soon.

They put us in a building near the square. As we went in, the guards finally looked through the bags we carried but removed nothing, even the fruit. We had no weapons, and that was all they cared about, though the phones drew some stares. I didn't think they'd seen anything like it, which meant no recent visitors.

Then they left us inside but kept guards at every door and window. I glimpsed more of them on their way up from the city.

Pillows lined one wall, and I took that as a good sign.

"We might as well rest," I told the others.

Tessa sat first and pushed a pillow under his ankle. He looked almost content.

"They've had no outside contact," Rose said with a worried shake of her head. "There is no sign of the modern world out there."

"They've seen some strangers, though," I offered. "You can tell it by the way they watched us."

"Strangers who never left again," Lily said, putting that much together. She looked panicked for the first time in her life. "They would have told someone about this place. My family!"

"I'm going to get us out of this," I told her. The Unholy Five stared at me with disbelief. "I can understand a lot of what they are saying. It's close to modern Quechan. Tessa has practiced it with me, too -- did you catch much of it?"

"Quite a bit," he admitted and seemed pleased with my answer of how we understood. "I heard nothing hostile, either."

"Neither did I." I started looking around the place. One curtained area turned out to be a bathroom of sorts. Good. I pointed it out to the others and then found another room with even more pillows and blankets. The single opening was high on the wall.

I shooed my sisters in there, and they didn't argue. Everyone looked exhausted by this point, and I hoped they would soon be asleep. Lily had tears in her eyes, and I thought Rose's eyes seemed a little bright as well. Violet appeared stoic

-- she always did, no matter what the situation. Carnation seemed to be shocked beyond any reasonable emotion. Aster just shook her head in disbelief, but she remained steady. She'd help the others.

That left Tessa and me alone in the outer room. We moved away from the wall, closer to my sisters, even though the walls were thick, and I didn't think they would hear us whispering. The guards could listen to us, but I doubted they spoke English. If they did -- well, we just wouldn't have any secrets.

Tessa settled with his back to the wall below the window. I brought a few pillows and helped him get comfortable. He nodded his thanks.

I couldn't see much but the edge of the plaza. This might be a home, and that they had cleared it out of anything we might use as a weapon. That was fine. They'd left Tessa with his cane, at least. I thought that meant they didn't take us too seriously.

"While I know why you did it," Tessa said as I settled by him. "You must stop wishing for things, Summerfield. Too soon again, and it will kill you. You got lucky that time -- you wished for something for yourself, and that was easier on your body. You might have asked for others to understand you -- and you would have been dead long before that wish spread through this city."

" My head pounded, but the rush of all the other emotions overpowered even the pain. "I might not have done it if I'd remembered about the fae and languages -- but I don't think it will hurt for the two of us to understand what's being said. I can't imagine we'll stay together for too long."

Tessa nodded. "What do you think is going on?"

"The mural explained how some of the ancestors to this group arrived on a Spanish slave ship. There might have been an earlier expedition -- oh. Remember about Pizarro and the raft? If he thought there had been more gold and silver on some island not far away, he would have sent a treasure ship to grab it as well."

Tessa nodded.

"I also have a theory of how they've stayed undetected. I think there is a shield over at least this part of the island."

"Ah." Tessa tilted his head back and looked up at the window. "Yes, I believe you're right."

"Even if search planes came looking, they'll miss us, Tessa. Our best hope is to get the notice of our people. Can we use the local magic to do it?"

"We must think about how to do it," he replied with a frown. "What should we expect, though?"

"I don't know yet. I tried to note different levels of society here. They do have slaves, Tessa. Don't snarl. In some ways, that's good for us. I'd rather spend some time as a slave than a sacrifice to their gods."

"Oh. Yes. Excellent point."

"I can tell you about Inca society at Spanish contact. There were nobles, commoners, and slaves. The nobles held the high-level priesthood plus the government and military posts. Our guards are Inca soldiers, so I think we can assume that's the basic structure here. I'm not sure about landowners. We saw no villages on our way here. I would suspect whoever rules here controls everything."

"And given the magic, I would say that would be the

priests."

"Very likely," I agreed. I could not see the temple from here, but I could feel the pulse of the power there. "These people haven't killed us outright. That means someone is curious, Tessa. Let's hope we can keep them interested. I still have faith in Brandis and the rest for getting us out."

CHAPTER 11

Sometime after noon, the guards ordered us to prepare to go to the temple. I filled my sisters in on what little Tessa and I thought we'd figured out and suggested that they should remain silent and obey as best as they could.

"Slavery," Violet had said, and for once, her eyes flashed with anger.

"Or sacrifices," I reminded her.

She took a deep breath as though she meant to argue with me -- and then let it go. "Yes. You're right. What a mess, Sunflower. But at least we have you to sort some of this out. What if we'd ended up here without you?"

That drew the attention of the others. They all looked startled and worried by that idea. I couldn't tell them they had crashed because of me and my link to Dagon, either.

"You would have done fine. I can't see where my knowing any of this will help us, except I can talk to the locals. Sometimes. If I mess that up, who knows what will happen? A single word that has changed in the cultural connotation could be worse than not understanding at all."

Then the guards said the Priestess demanded our attendance. I didn't care for the wording, but that could be her usual address to people outside the temple. It was not something to make any complaint over.

Tessa and I went in the lead this time, the other five following us in a line. It wasn't as though we would lose them along the way, so I did my best not to look back.

Inca temples had ramps, not staircases. Parrots of various colors flew by, yelling at our intrusion. We went up one ramp and a second -- and there we waited.

The Priestess and her four people came from the building high atop the temple. She seemed only a flash of blue feathers and a golden mask in the shape of a jaguar's face. This was the first sign of gold I'd seen on the island. I wondered if it might not be ancient and from another place.

She stared at us. "You are strange," she mumbled.

"Priestess," I said with a bow of my head. "We mean you and your people no harm."

I think no one had told her that Tessa and I spoke Quechan. My words took her so much by surprise that she stepped back in shock. Her priests and the soldiers all brought up weapons, and I thought we were all going to die of her astonishment.

She lifted a hand and stopped them. I dared to breathe again.

"You are wonders," she said and looked down at my group from a little height up the ramp. Maybe we should have knelt, but it was too late now for such formalities. "We have seen others as pale, but none who could speak with us. They never survived, either."

Yes, that was a warning. I gave a bow of my head and tried not to get sidetracked by two quipocamayos -- men who were tying the knots in the long strings of khipus. Some experts had said the khipus represented nothing more than the record-keeping for numbers, or at best a memory aid -- but I thought he recorded the history of this meeting, and if I could learn how to read --

I tore my attention away from the khipus to the Priestess. She had lifted her hand, long-fingered hand festooned with jeweled rings and gold bangles on her wrists. The fingers twitched from me to Tessa and back. She made no sound, but I sensed a frown behind the mask.

"No others who have come to us have had power as you two do," she said. Tessa made a little sound of worry. "Yes, I can feel it. You will grant that power to me."

Well, there was going to be a problem.

"It is not ours to give," Tessa replied. He'd kept quiet until now, and I was glad to have him take over this part of the discussion. I understood the basics of the situation, but this was something Tessa might say far better than I could in my growing sense of panic.

"You do not tell me the truth," she said with a tilt of her head. I saw a hunger in those dark eyes, half-hidden behind her golden mask. "You two are the ones with power, though. Guards, take the women away. Find what work they can do."

I dared a glance back at my sisters. "Go where they say and follow orders. Be wise and wait. We will figure this out."

A warrior hit me across the shoulder with the staff of his spear. It was not hard, but the blow drew my attention. The Priestess frowned at me, but she turned to Tessa.

"You are the one who has the actual power. His is different. Does he do your bidding?"

There was a trick question, and one I needed to answer

with extreme care. It had everything to do with power levels. I decided to take a chance.

"I speak for Tessa as you speak for the Sapa Inca."

Yes, that startled her. She almost stepped down to our level and caught herself in time. That would have been a mistake on her part.

"Others of your kind have never known us so well."

I glanced at Tessa and even bowed my head to him. "Tessa will speak if it is important. I handle other matters."

As I had hoped, the arrangement made sense to her. Tessa looked calm, too. I thought we had reached a level of understanding as far as ranks went. Could I dare ask for my sisters to return?

Perhaps it would be better if they were not so close to us at this critical time. This was a delicate match of power-to-power -- and neither Tessa nor I could show any magic. But then, neither had she.

Clouds began billowing up over the ocean, though. I sensed another tremendous storm coming our way with an underlying hint of frustration yet again.

"The storms follow you," the Priestess said with a frown. "You bring danger and destruction."

"Illapa brings the storms," I countered. Tessa would need to learn the names of the Gods as soon as possible. "We have no control over such beings. What have you done to displease Illapa?"

I saw a quick rush of emotions at that statement, read in the shift of her body even if I couldn't see her face beyond the jaguar mask. I had surprised her, maybe just knowing the name of the God. She wasn't at all happy with the idea that

Illapa might be unhappy with her. She stared at the clouds again.

"Take them back," she said and turned to leave.

Tessa and I both bowed to her. The Priestess seemed a little surprised and pleased. Good. If we kept her confused, that might help us survive.

Tessa's ankle must hurt. He leaned on the makeshift cane, but he kept his face clear of any sign of pain. He knew about power plays far better than I did. I thought we had done well enough, though.

We went back to our rooms. My sisters were not there, but someone had brought food and water. We sat down and ate and sipped, but neither of us spoke at first. I served Tessa -- I would have anyway, given his injury. The guards looked in now and then, and once a priest even came by and stared. I had expected him to come inside. He did not.

The rain fell, and the winds roared through the town. I worried about the Unholy Five, but we dared not say anything to make them essential and noticeable. I considered suggesting they were Tessa's wives -- but I still suspected that we didn't want them that much in our circle of attention.

They showed up, wet and annoyed, just before the storm broke loose with more rain.

"We learned the fine art of grinding corn," Aster said and held up blistered fingers when they gathered in the back of the room. "Oh, it could be much worse. The other women taught us out. We just worried about what had happened to the two of you."

"A few more words with the Priestess, but I don't think it helped," Tessa said. We shared the food around.

I could hear people outside yelling about the rain. I supposed they were having trouble with flooding, so I went to the door to check out the area. Water streamed by across the stone inlay of the road and heading down toward the bay. I nodded to the soldiers on either side of the door.

"Step inside to guard if it grows dangerous," I said. I didn't wait to see their answers. I'd made the offer.

We gathered far back from the opening. I told the others more about the Inca and their Gods and all I could come up with until my voice grew rough and the light faded. I could not tell them enough. In fact, I feared that I didn't know adequate information despite all my odd life and education.

"Rest, Sunflower," Rose ordered at last. "You've told us more than we can take in already."

She was right. I'd veered a little too close to magic. Tessa looked as though he was contemplating a lot of what I'd said. Good. He would have to talk to the Priestess on his own at some point.

I laid down and listened to the rain and the thunder. Lightning brightened the area now and then. The others had all gone to sleep. I thought that wise and wished I could do the same. After all, this was a lovely, solid building. We hadn't been out of the weather lately. The roof, made of pottery, provided a dull whisper of sound as the rain washed over it. A single small leak trickled a little water at the edge of one wall. I wanted to study the architecture and to go out and walk the streets.

I did not want to sleep and miss anything.

Then I worried that I'd have all the time in the world to study this place, for all the good it would do me if we would not escape. I had to push that thought back with a reminder that Brandis, Kala, Vane -- Arinith, and even the Queen of the fae -- would search by now.

Someone among them would notice this little spot of magic. That would draw them in. Why haven't they found us yet?

A glance at Tessa showed him twitching in his sleep. I felt as though I was the only one awake in the world, a guardian against ... I didn't know what. When I fell off to sleep, my dreams circled and twisted with hints of Spanish, Incan, and Aztec images. Dagon appeared, of course, and his power shook everything and woke me again.

The rain had eased. I went closer to the window, drawing a muffled sound from Tessa.

I looked out at the town. The guards remained in place. One looked my way and then paid no attention at all.

I couldn't see much, which I found frustrating, there in the dark -- ah, but then I noticed something. A slight bluish glow came from the direction of the volcano -- no, not the volcano. The light came from lower, at the temple's level and just looking at it gave me a chill. That was the first full sign of magic I'd seen here. I almost called Tessa over to see, but I realized that would be a waste of his resting time.

What the hell had we wandered into? Had Dagon pushed us here? I thought about the storms again. The first, while we'd been on the plane, had felt like anger to me. I'd gotten to know the touch of his power.

These last, though, hinted more frustration. Perhaps we were not where Dagon wanted. Or maybe I had survived when he didn't want me to. If we got out of this, I needed to do something about the trouble with him.

That meant dealing with the Priestess, who worried that other gods showed displeasure with her. I had not asked whom she served. An Incan god or a Aztec one? Now that I could sit in the quiet of the night and call back the scenes, I realized that I had seen symbols of both pantheons.

Too damned many questions.

I tried to sleep, but that didn't work very well, and by dawn, I was the one who had slept the least and needed it the most to make sense of this world.

I didn't know what to expect.

CHAPTER 12

The next morning a group of slaves -- three men and two women -- brought us more food and drink. Their own guards watched, and no one spoke. I made a sign for the others to keep silent. Talking to slaves would be trouble on many levels.

None of the group serving us looked like they were from the Incan or Aztec people. They might be castaways. I feared that I was looking at our futures if any of us survived.

Guards led my sisters out of the building a little later. I heard something about working the fields, and I hoped they did well. Then they took Tessa and me out, but they parted us at the edge of the pyramid. Tessa went up the two ramps and no higher while I remained behind and under guard. I couldn't hear what he and the Priestess said. The woman glanced my way more than once, and I wished I could advise Tessa on what to say.

Instead, I studied the pyramid. I had not noticed the decoration the last time, being too worried that we would not survive to come back down. I could see almost all of one line of murals. They again combined Inca and Aztec motifs. Quetzalcoatl, the ubiquitous Mesoamerica serpent god, appeared more often than any of the others. What brought this group to take in the Winged Serpent? Then I remembered the mural with the statue that the Spanish had been transporting. Maybe it had survived when none of the other relics of their own Gods had reached this shore.

The Priestess waved her hand. The guards took me away. I glanced once at Tessa, who gave a rather regal nod toward me as the warriors led me back to the rooms.

They'd blocked off the road by the building so that no one came near except unless the guards let them pass.

There I remained, alone.

I don't do well on my own. I get annoyed and worried. My imagination gives me every dangerous scenario that could happen beyond my reach. What happened if Tessa died here? Would we lose the Cat Clan totem?

And my sisters. What if they didn't survive, and I had to tell their families? A dozen children. Four husbands. My grandparents. My parents --

I sat down and stared at the wall for a while. Excellent brickwork. Not the megalithic stuff I'd seen in Cuzco, but some of it reminded me of Machu Picchu. The Inca had always had a fine touch for building, and this group must have brought some artisans and kept hold of that tradition.

And others, as well. Weavers? Pottery makers? I wondered how much it would take to keep a small scattering of people alive long enough to even begin a civilization that had grown to this place. The city looked magnificent, and I wished I could enjoy it.

I heard the odd sound of bells and realized they grew louder as they neared. A half dozen priests walked ahead of the Priestess, but they all waited outside while she came through the door. The guards took positions at the doorway and the window with their spears raised as I stood.

She did not wear the jaguar mask this time, and I could see that her face looked lean, long-nosed -- more like the mask than I had expected, though.

"I would stay there on your knees if I were you," she warned with a twitch of her lips that was not an actual smile.

I bowed my head in agreement.

Then she asked me questions and appeared quite shocked at how much I knew about the Inca. I even dared a few Aztec references and won more surprise. I hoped I could at least keep her intrigued.

"You know more than the Tessa."

"It is my job to know more," I said.

It was the right answer.

"Where is Tessa?" I dared to ask.

"Oh, somewhere safe for now. I do not think I can trust the two of you together. You have powers, and will you give them with me?"

"They are not mine to share," I replied with a bow of my head.

"Another refusal." Her voice had gone a little hard.

I realized something I had not noticed when we were on the temple, that bastion of power that both Tessa and I had felt. The Priestess had powers of her own. She radiated magic, though not the fae type. I was used to sensing such things and had not taken note the day before.

So why did she want our magic? Was it a fear that we could take over? Or was it a need to replenish her own magic? Could I play on that theme and promise her something that I couldn't give to her?

I feared that might play too tricky of a game for Karma.

"Perhaps, there is another you should see," the Priestess said as she leaned a little closer to stare into my eyes. "Since I have been in the presence of the one you attend, you shall stand before he whom I serve."

Sapa Inca? Oh, I was not ready for that kind of meeting. I knew nothing about the protocol for the most high-ranking member of the Inca society.

But I couldn't say no, could I?

I bowed my head again and stood when she signaled me. She went back out. The priests moved with her, and the Eagle Warriors pressed in around me.

We did not go to the temple, which didn't surprise me. Instead, took the long main road through the city to an open square. In the middle of the open area sat an ornate building with an odd tower. I'd not seen this sort of structure before. The Jaguar Warriors stood at this entrance, which meant they served the Sapa Inca while the Eagle Warriors served the Priestess. I had not expected that kind of demarcation. I wondered if this was a change from the society they'd left on the mainland or if it was just something we'd never discerned in the ruins of their homelands.

The Priestess, one of the Jaguar Warriors, and I went inside. I didn't like the tight walls or the odd symbols everywhere. A gallery of statues representing the Incan Gods stood just above my head on both sides. Their faces hid in the shadows, though the eyes still stared down at us. A single spot of light shown far down the corridor. The place remained eerily quiet. Our footsteps moved on old stone; the path had worn down through the ages. This was a path where many walked, but the place still had the feel of emptiness.

Of death. I should have realized we were going to face a mummy.

The Sapa Inca sat wrapped in several layers of cloth. He wore an ornate golden crown on his sunken skin and long black hair laid across his shoulders and feathered out around him. I stared at his face and wondered if he had been dead before they brought him here.

"Kneel before Atahualpa," the Priestess growled, and the guard struck me with his spear.

Atahualpa had been the last Sapa Inca before Pizarro executed him. I knelt in awe, in fact. He'd ruled over a vast empire, although he fought his brother in a civil war that weakened the Inca before the Spanish Conquest. He had seen his people prosperous and happy until the Spanish arrived.

Had he brought his blessings here where a remnant of his followers -- and a few Aztec -- survived? Pizzaro and his priests had believed they'd destroyed all the Inca mummies, but this one escaped to remain venerated.

Good? Bad? It didn't matter in such a unique situation.

The Priestess took me back out of the tomb, and I felt better for being out into the light, even with the worry of more storms.

"Where is Tessa?" I asked again. She expected it. That I didn't ask about the Sapa Inca and made it evident that I knew many things about him and the Inca bothered her.

She ignored me. She gave a single nod, and the guards led me off to work with the slaves in some nearby fields, no doubt showing me what life would be like if I didn't cooperate.

Maybe she even believed me the weaker of the two since my magic wouldn't appear as robust as Tessa's.

I helped harvest potatoes, which I found amusing, since I'd done the same when I'd still traveled with my parents, so many long years ago in South America.

The tiered fields amazed me. I studied them the best I could and (silently) wished I had a pen and paper to make notes and do drawings. I refused to believe that I would work here for the rest of my life. With that thought, this became a unique study of an ancient civilization.

Off to the right, I spotted a field of corn -- but no, not just corn. They were growing the Three Sisters -- squash at the base of the corn to protect the soil, corn to grow tall, and beans that curled up the corn stalk. The plants produced small ears -- they didn't have the huge mutant cobs we grew in Nebraska.

The Three Sisters were a more northern custom, though. Like the blending of Aztec and Incan symbols, many things seemed out of place here. I indexed them in my mind.

Then I spotted Carnation and Lily working the field not far away, dressed in local clothing, and neither looked happy. That brought me back to reality. I saw no sign of the others, including Tessa. I tried to get closer to Lily, but she didn't see me, and the overseer dissuaded me from trying again with a quick flick of his quirt.

No, not a pleasant place, even if I found it intriguing. Rage rose when I realized they might use that quirt on my sisters. I fought the emotion back down and concentrated on what I was doing, the simple wooden tools we used, and the words spoken around me. I heard some Spanish. If I got alone with some slaves, we could talk. Had they all been here their entire lives? Did some come from elsewhere? Did they have family legends about other lands?

Did they have families?

Once I started down the rabbit hole of questions, there was no coming back. I did my work, but everything just piled up in untidy stacks in my mind, and I despaired more that I wouldn't figure it out rather than about not getting away.

I wanted to talk to Tessa. He had been around for a long time and might have some ideas about dealing with these people.

I didn't dare consider that I had lost Tessa. I wouldn't want to return to the fae if I couldn't bring the Cat Clan totem back with me.

That fear won an adverse reaction from me, despite my attempts to stay calm. I looked around in a panicked turn. The quirt came down again. I almost acted in anger, but then I saw Lily looking my way, frantic and worried.

With some effort, I regained my control. I thought about this strange place I'd fallen into and not about everything that could go wrong. By now, most of the fae would have already started searching for us. I had faith that my people would find us before too long.

Though maybe not soon enough. I had forgotten about Dagon, but he knew where to find me. When the day grew dark, I heard shouts of worry everywhere in the city.

I looked up and saw a massive gray cloud that appeared to have spread over the sky in a matter of moments. Lightning flashed, and thunder shook the ground a moment later. Then the rains came with such a deluge that I feared all of us, including the plants, were going to wash down the hillsides.

We had to divert the water, or they'd lose their crops. I knew who would suffer if the locals lost some of the food supply. The slaves were all thinner than anyone else I'd spotted so far. I also noted that there could not be more than a few hundred of them, either. They would be a simple group to destroy and then replace from the lowest level of the free population. If I were any of those locals, I'd worry about disasters.

Not this time, though. I looked around, recalling Inca fields and floods back in Peru. We had to move fast, and the overseer wasn't happy with me directing others to make little dikes at the base of each plant, to dig deeper at one end and direct the water downhill along a single path --

Soon, however, the man moved with me from terrace to terrace as I directed the others. News of what we were doing spread, and what had been despair not long before became hope again.

The downpour continued, but we had several fields in hand already. I had slipped too many times, and my knee throbbed, but I limped along, clearing debris where we needed to, pointing out more spots to shore up the terraces. The locals were used to a lot of rain in this area, but not so much as they were getting since I arrived.

When the storm blew up again, I turned into the wind and scowled. "Dagon, you don't want to annoy me anymore! You may think I'm helpless, but I will not be here forever."

Lightning struck the ground a few yards away to my right, sending an unpleasant jolt through the water-logged soil. Others gave cries of fear, and even the overseer retreated in haste. I stood alone on the terrace, though looking across the valley, I spotted people at the temple. That would be the Priestess, and she watched me.

The wind blew harder. Lightning stuck to the left side of me this time, and between the flash of light, the jolt of power, and the explosive boom, I should have gone down, but I stood my ground.

Dagon helped me, though I doubted that had been his intent. I had shouted in English, and I supposed that sounded as much like an incantation as Latin might seem to others. I had withstood the storm and perhaps even called lightning to me. Dagon made me look stronger, but I didn't want him to stick around.

"You will not kill me," I shouted into the growing wind. "If you do, then you go back to your crumbling temple. I am your link to the world. Unless you want to sleep again, you had better stop annoying me. I may not have the power to do anything against you right now, but that will change."

The wind lessened. Thunder came like the growl of an unhappy dog, and the clouds dispersed. A rainbow formed over the ocean, a pretty parting sign as the sudden storm swept away and disappeared again.

Dagon would not accept this latest insult to his dignity. I had more than enough to worry about without the addition of an ancient god who did not belong in this setting at all.

By turning the storm, I had proven my powers. I knew that wasn't good, either. Or maybe it was since it kept the Priestess guessing.

I glanced at where she stood, but the woman had turned and headed inside the upper-level temple. Even from here, I could see her disapproval and knew that was not good news for me.

The slaves, though, appeared happier. I looked around and spotted my sisters. They worked far enough away not to have heard what I said -- I hoped. I'd have to say I was playing at their games and pretending I had powers. Yeah. Right.

Facing down an ancient Assyrian God had been tiring. And my leg ached now -- but it was not time to retire. The slaves went back to work, but a group of men came and asked me questions about drainage. We worked on the system for the rest of the afternoon.

I felt Dagon on the breeze now and then, testing the area as though he thought he might try again. Except for threats, I had no power against him. He didn't know me well enough to realize how the idea of banishing him back to sleep bothered me. That reluctance had to do with my background and all the wonders I'd seen. Dagon was a power that had once held an essential place in the world, and sometimes I thought we were no better for having pushed all those Old Gods out. Even so, there was a lot about Dagon's ruthlessness that I didn't like, either. I suppose that I still hoped to tame him somehow.

Dagon began to wear on my nerves.

At one point, Lily drew close enough to speak to me.

"We saw what you did in the storm. Are you crazy?" Lily demanded.

"I thought you'd already decided about that issue -- and that's what got us into this mess."

She was not happy with my answer, but she moved away again before an overseer came our way.

We worked until sunset, a spectacular glow of red, orange, and pink across the darkening and cloud-dotted sky. I followed the others down off the terraces, trying not to trip on the uneven ground. My leg hurt, but it wasn't more than a nasty twist. If I had a day or two of rest, it would be fine.

Somehow, I didn't expect that to happen.

They didn't take me back to the pleasant house in town. Instead, they herded me along to a set of huts at the base of the hills, in a swampy, half-flooded area. Water still stood in pools here, but the buildings sat on stilts. Small children, too young to work, came out of a hut where they had stayed during the day. Weary parents gathered them up. Single men went one way, and unmarried women went the other. I nodded to Lily and Carnation as they walked away with the women, which included my other sisters, too. I felt a wave of relief to see them at all.

We had no chance to talk. Guards watched while other slaves brought food to each hut.

I didn't care as I choose a spot with no mat or other sign that someone had claimed the location, and I laid down and went to sleep.

Then I woke up not too much later, feeling groggy and bad-tempered. Someone tried to give me a tortilla wrapped around what smelled like peppers and perhaps beans. I snarled something impolite.

"Take it. Eat it now, or the bugs will get at it," the man said, and in English.

That drew all my attention. "Who the hell are you?" I asked, startled enough to sit up.

In the dim light, I saw a tall man -- tan, pale-haired, and

gray-eyed. He dressed in the locals' style, but I could tell this was not someone who had been born to his current station.

"I'm Paul Carter," he said, his eyes hooded and distrusting.

"Summerfield," I replied, and he frowned a little. "SB Summerfield. How long have you been here?"

"Years. At least three. Maybe more, I don't know. I went crazy for a while." He spoke with a flickering look around, hinting that perhaps crazy had inched closer again. I thought about being here for as long as Paul while hope that someone would find him dwindling with each odd day. "You get used to it after a while."

I didn't believe him. He lied to himself, but I understood that part.

"This is a strange place," I admitted. I ate some of the spicy food. It reminded me of home. "I've trained in archeology, so I recognize things that don't belong together."

"Inca, Aztec," he said with a nod. "I figured that out. But the Spanish took them both down about the same time, right? So maybe it's not so strange."

Paul gave me someone to talk to who was not one of my sisters. He'd been here long enough that he might have noticed stuff I wanted to understand, too.

"I've seen some other influence as well. This is like the land of lost civilizations."

"An experiment," Paul replied with a growl. "There's no way someone doesn't know about this, and that means they've left us here on purpose, the bastards!"

His voice had grown louder. Two men urged him to quiet. The last light of day silhouetted a dozen men in the small building. The others sat and ate in silence. A guard walked by outside and watched for a moment before he moved on.

I thought the guards didn't understand any of the languages that the slaves spoke. That would make them uneasy.

I ate more of the food and considered what Paul had said. He had found his own logical reason rescue had never arrived. I didn't dissuade him of it. What would happen if I found a way out? What about everyone else, from slave to elite, if this place showed up on the map?

Part of me didn't want to ruin the civilization here. I considered all the information we could learn about that the passage of time and fanatics had destroyed on the mainland.

But there were actual people like Paul trapped in this place. What about the Priestess who presented a unique problem because she had magic? Paul must have seen signs of that power -- ah, but I guessed how he would have explained that one.

"Is the Priestess the one in charge of everything?" I dared to ask.

"That bitch," he mumbled, but quieter. "Yeah. She has most everyone cowed with some devices she keeps up in the temple. I figure she must have communications equipment and stuff up there to give reports."

I had been right. Technology could explain the magic. He stopped and nibbled at his food, then gave me a sidelong look, almost lost in the growing darkness.

"Damned devoted to this project, too. I've never seen her leave."

"It's all strange," I said and didn't challenge his vision of the world. I found it far more appealing than my own just then.

I ate the bread, drank a little water from the common bucket, and went back to sleep. Paul moved off to his own place. He mumbled a few things in Spanish to the others, but I didn't care.

I had an odd dream that night. Not a surprise, but this was one of those dreams that might have had a link to my strange version of reality. Dagon glared at me, but I could tell he appeared troubled rather than mad. Something had changed, and I'd missed the transition. When he glanced over his shoulder, I looked as well. Someone else stood there, in the shadows. For a moment, I caught a quick glance of a face. I recognized the large round eyes, fanged teeth, and enormous nose. Chac, the Mayan rain God -- or perhaps Tlaloc, the Aztec deity who closely resembled him.

Had Dagon stepped on another God's toes, maybe even waking some in the process? Perhaps he'd drawn out more than one considering the number of cultures we dealt with here.

Well, damn. That would mean more trouble for me because of my tie to Dagon. The others would realize it and consider me his avatar on earth and someone who had invaded their realm.

That's the type of problem I faced so often that I didn't even have to think too hard about how this could go from being Dagon's bad manners to my problem. I did not know what to do, either.

I woke to the shout of someone at the door. The others

scrambled up, and I let myself get caught up in the rush, following Paul out into the faint light of dawn. We marched to the latrine -- I'd be redesigning that place if I stuck around here for long -- and then through a line where women gave us some papaya. I glanced at the temple. Priests as they headed inside the building at the top of the pyramid.

I realized that was a larger structure than would have been typical in any of the cultures I'd seen represented here. Maybe that one went back to Moche times? Maybe Olmec? We knew little about either of those people. Why limit this strange place to just two groups? For all I knew, the survivors from the Spanish ship might have found others here already.

Yeah, I could still look at things that way, even though I felt tired, my leg hurt, and I wanted pancakes, eggs, sausage --

Oh, best not to think about anything like that right now.

We hiked up to a different set of terraces this time as they took me to work on the drainage system in other areas. I thought about either telling them to go to hell or else negotiating to get my sisters and Tessa back.

I decided that neither was a good idea. At this moment, I had about as much cooperation as I would get from these people. They didn't want to deal with me -- I could see that in their faces. If I gave them any trouble, they'd give up on the improvements, and I'd be with no influence at all. Knowledge is power -- that may be a cliché, but it provided me with some leverage.

I crawled around on my aching knee and did the work, answering the questions some asked as politely as I could. I sneezed a few times, too. Not a surprise that I had a cold coming on, given what we'd all gone through of late.

Some elites came to watch, stayed for a short while, and then went back to their shaded homes, leaving slaves and overseers to keep working. I didn't count the number of terraces I would have to visit. I showed other slaves how to do the job, and that would help spread it out. Good, because I felt like hell now. I had a scratch in my throat and my eyes watered. My hands trembled, and a couple times, I just couldn't get up to my feet.

This would not be my favorite vacation after all.

In the late morning, I heard a sound that gave me hope for the first time since the plane crashed.

A large cat yowled, and somewhere nearby. I'd been kneeling in the mud, and I got to my feet. Tessa --

And then a second cat yowled, and I saw how everyone else had gone still and stared up at the edge of the jungle that towered over us. Something moved, and then a capybara darted out into the open. The large animal charged straight into the fields, running for his life.

Two jaguars followed, gorgeous and lethal -- and all three headed straight at me. I threw myself at the base of the wall of the terrace above me. The capybara leapt off, tangled in some plants, and kept going. The jaguars remained so engrossed in the chase that they never saw me, though they passed within a few feet.

Several men followed, and I realized they were ocelomeh -- Aztec's elite Jaguar Warriors. They wore jaguar skins and carrying macuahuitls. Those dangerous obsidian-lined wooden clubs could kill with a single blow. I thought they were hunting the jaguars, but then I realized they hunted with the cats. From the surge of fear that I saw in my companions, these animals might attack anyone.

Jaguar Warriors had been the front-line soldiers in Aztec wars. I thought they must have a different function here. They looked no less deadly for it.

The jaguars chased after their original prey, destroying parts of the terraces and heading into the city below. I could hear sounds of panic even there. The Jaguar Warriors proved no better than the animals, and I didn't have to look at the others to know that I should remain still. Besides, this was the longest rest I'd had all day.

We did our best to fix the damage once the chase moved on. My hands trembled, and I looked back at the temple more than once. Priests moved in and out. I spotted the Priestess once --, and yes, she stared in my direction.

I did not see Tessa and hoped he turned up soon and told me he'd found an answer to get around our stupid oath. Tessa with magic, and Tessa turning into a cat, might just keep us safe.

We got a noon meal that day. Older women and young girls carted out several bowls, which they dipped into a larger container and passed around a plain corn gruel. Violet and Rose worked with those who brought the food. I almost hadn't recognized them in the simple tunic-like dress of the locals, and both with their hair so untidy. I wondered why the Unholy Five had to wear local attire, but not me. Was it because they were female? Or was it because they had no sign of magic? My clothing made me simple to spot. I thought the Priestess might appreciate having that way to find me.

Both of my sisters looked as relieved as I was to see them. I knew we had little time, but the overseers did not stop the slaves from talking to each other, so I took the chance.

"You're alright?" I all but whispered and even dared a hand on Rose's arm.

"Easier work than you, Carnation, and Lily. Aster is with us, too. What the hell have we fallen into, Sunflower?"

I did not wince at the name. At least no one would understand -- but then I spotted Paul nearby with an amused look. Well, I supposed he could use a little humor these days.

"Have you seen Tessa at all?"

"Aster thought she saw him in the temple yesterday. She wasn't sure since he dressed in fancy robes."

I nodded. "I'm working on the problem."

Rose understood that we dared not linger. She and Violet moved on. I wanted to ask questions, but I ate my food in silence and passed the bowl -- wooden, hand-carved, and worn smooth by the years -- back to the girl who came to collect it.

Not much later, Eagle Warriors from the Priestess arrived and collected me. I had thought the Priestess's patience wouldn't hold out much longer. Besides, the weather looked better today, and she might want to get to a discussion before the next storm. I did not imagine she enjoyed being out in the rain.

Before I ascended the temple, servants threw buckets of scented water over me. I sneezed and wasn't sure if that came from a cold or from allergies. I stood in the warm sun and dried off somewhat before they prodded me back up the ramp.

My knee hurt and got worse. I wondered if I should wish it better -- and then realized that would be a dangerous move. I did not want to show any outward magic anywhere near the

Priestess. Besides, I didn't feel well, and losing the power to fuel that odd magic might just drop me unconscious at her feet.

Also, not a good idea.

"You have helped the people," the woman said, and with no preamble. "Why?"

"Working on the drainage?" I dared to ask and won a curt nod. "Because it helps others. I knew some things that would save more of the crops. Why shouldn't I help?"

She snarled, and her eyes narrowed. Afraid for her position and prestige? That could make me a dangerous person, but since I showed no magic --

Except I had confronted a storm, and it had gone away again.

Damn.

I had thought that would help give me more status, but I hadn't considered how that status would conflict with the Priestess's position. I answered her questions about crops and floods. She asked about magic. I said nothing helpful, and she grew angry.

"You will help the slaves, but not me," she snarled. "What can they give you?"

"Honor."

Oh, not my wisest answer. The woman's eyes widened, and her hand twitched. I thought I would have a less than honorable death, but she didn't follow through with the order. Instead, she turned and went up to the temple. The guards escorted me downward. I almost fell twice, and they had to half carry me at the end. They did not take me to the fields because it was already so late in the day, and it would just be more trouble getting me up and back down again.

I had a little time in the hut alone, so I slept and woke when the others arrived, turned away from the food, and slept some more. Nightmares made the sleep far from helpful. Paul tried to talk to me, but if I answered, I doubted it made sense.

By dawn, the worst of the fever had passed. I went back to the terraces and kept a worried watch on the skies. Desperation brought darker thoughts. My clan should have located me by now. Did they not even realize that the two of us had disappeared? My sisters had told them I was going off on a surprise vacation. Tessa? Tessa just wandered off sometimes for a few days. We hadn't disappeared so long ago yet. It might take a few more days.

Weeks? Months?

I looked up at the sky and watched clouds massing again, and I couldn't say I cared.

CHAPTER 13

On day seven, I looked around, amazed at how well I had adjusted to the new life. I hadn't accepted it, but I did my work with no trouble. I listened to what the others said in the hut at night and kept mental notes for a future paper I might never write. Most of my companions wanted to take a wife, make a family. This was all the world they knew, and they nurtured their dreams within the framework of their society.

On the tenth day, we had a rest from the fields while the city celebrated a festival. The slaves didn't take part, but we didn't work, either. We had our own little feast and gathered on a small knoll near the huts. I talked with my sisters. I'd never seen them so happy to see me.

"This is Paul," I said with a nod to the man who spent time with me, sharing a language that no one else understood. "He's a late-comer to this paradise, too."

"We are so sorry, Sunflower," Aster whispered.

I sighed and gave up on trying to stop them from using that name. Instead, I introduced the Unholy Five to Paul Carter. By the end, he smiled.

"So, Sunflower really is your name!"

"I prefer Summerfield," I said. "But, yes, that is my name. Sunflower Breeze Summerfield. Go ahead and snicker.

Someone ought to get some enjoyment out of it."

I grinned, though. Paul laughed. I thought a little of the stress went out of him. Paul acted like a man on the verge of doing something stupid soon. I wasn't sure I could stop him, either.

"We've learned some strange things, Kid," Rose said, using a name somewhat better than Sunflower. We all sat on the knoll, away from the worst of the swamplands, and where even the bugs did not bother us much. At least it hadn't rained so often the last week. "They all speak an odd form of Spanish. I assume you've caught that with your affinity for languages."

"Yes. I believe the slaves worked hard to keep all the elite's language out of theirs. It's the only form of privacy they have."

She nodded. "All the women have been born to this island, and as far as they're concerned, this and the ocean is all there is to the world."

"Ana told me a myth about a ship that brought their ancestors," Aster added. She nibbled at some pineapple and looked worn. "And the octopus that destroyed it, but she may have learned the tale from the mosaics."

"That could be true," I agreed, though I supposed it amounted to the same thing. I glanced at Paul, who frowned but said nothing.

"You have no idea how sorry we are that we dragged you into this," Aster added. "It was stupid --"

"Hold that thought until we're back home where I can exploit it properly," I replied and won a surprised snort from Violet. I don't think she'd ever made such a sound in her life.

But that brought laughter to all the Flowers.

"There is one more odd thing we've heard," Lily added. Her voice dropped. "They say the Priestess and her followers will never die because they worship each morning and draw power from the temple. The women swear the Priestess and her top priests are the same people who have been here since the beginning."

Paul shook his head but looked toward the pyramid with a frown. He hadn't been here long enough to note anything that unusual. Besides, he never considered magic, either. Neither did my sisters, but I could tell from Aster's attitude that this 'myth' bothered her a great deal.

For me, though, the possibility made a little more sense of the place. Someone had taken control from the start. Besides, even now, I could feel magic in the temple at the top of the pyramid.

The Priestess and her people renewed their power each morning? What sort of magical object did they have inside there? Incan, Mayan, Aztec -- something else?

The day of peace gave me time to think. My sisters hovered over me and said that I needed rest. Paul wandered off and threw dice with the men. I wondered what they gambled for and who had introduced the game. Dicing struck me as a slave pastime, and I would find no sign of it in the city. The slaves could adapt and change, and the other levels of society could not. *Dared not.* Their entire society held on to a past that had disappeared centuries before in the rest of the world.

But the Priestess -- she wanted our powers. Why? Was her source dying out after so long? Or did she just lust after something that would give her new controls?

No matter what, neither Tessa nor I would let her link back to the Fae World.

From the knoll, I could see most of the city. The population, including the slaves, couldn't be over 30,000. The island itself might be as much as a hundred square miles, there wasn't much of it under cultivation.

Was the population outgrowing the fields and terraces? Did the Priestess need more power to expand to other areas? I considered what it would take to rule this place as I laid back on the mossy ground and slept. People talked around me in many languages, and I found that pleasant.

For a moment, I thought I heard Brandis trying to call to me. I started to answer him --

And the world trembled.

I came awake with a start, hearing startled cries throughout the city. Everyone had turned toward the north, and there the volcano belched out a plume of gray ash. The Priestess appeared on the temple's pyramid. For the first time, I felt a rush of power from her. A moment later, the world calmed again.

Well.

The quake had not been strong, but there must have been some damage to the temple. Slaves did not go to work on it, though. The priests set to do the repairs even before the Priestess went back inside. I felt the slight buzz of power from them, too.

The Sapa Inca did not *reside* within those walls. What was more important to them that they kept housed within that sacred building?

The Priestess sent for me. I'd rested well and made it up the steps with no trouble. She didn't wear the mask and looked worn, which didn't surprise me considering the amount of magic she'd used.

Eagle Warriors came up the pyramid with Tessa, who wore a local tunic but still had his pants and boots. I tried not to grin because I didn't want the Priestess to realize the depth to which she might use Tessa to manipulate me -- and the opposite.

"I have provided both of you with time to consider your choices," she said and leaned forward, her eyes bright. "Now either you give me your magic, or you both die."

"I have already told you that we cannot give the powers we have," Tessa replied. He had a grim look on his face. "And you can't steal them, either."

He put a hand to his arm. I hadn't noticed the bandage there, and I didn't like the implications.

I felt another wave of magic; it didn't come from her.

Tessa looked toward the temple with a start. What did they have in there?

I had to think fast, but my brain focused on the Warriors who took hold of me and forced me down to my knees. Tessa's face grew dark with rage. The executioner drew a toomi blade from his belt -- a special Inca knife made to decapitate people.

I turned my head away from Tessa --

"Summerfield!" Tessa yelled, and I could hear him struggling with the guards. "Wish for something!"

Yes! "I wish --"

I had no time to say more.

The ground shook with enough force to knock everyone off their feet, and the damned blade missed me by inches. The volcano gave an angry howl and this time ash, pumice, and rock shot up amid a glow of lava across the open sky. The cone cracked and molten stone boiled out in a bright red line.

Everyone panicked.

I'd already been on my knees and didn't tumble like the others while the stones swayed beneath us. I grabbed Tessa's arm and propelled him down and to the left. We dared not run for the city where we would be too easy to grab. We would head into the jungle, at least long enough to come up with a plan.

My sisters?

I hoped they would be wise and do fine without us. The Priestess hadn't focused on them since they had no magical powers. I had no intention of abandoning them, even if we found a way off the island, though. Tessa and I just needed time to regroup and rethink our plans. There had to be something in this conglomerate culture I could use to our benefit.

When I looked back, the Priestess and her followers still worked to calm the volcano. The amount of magic she used blanketed the area. I could feel her trying to soothe the fiery monster.

No wonder she wanted more power. We would have helped if we could have drawn on our magic, whether or not we liked her.

I fell partway down the pyramid, slid and rolled, and came back to my feet with Tessa's help. We'd reached the bottom, and he pulled me off toward the trees.

The ground continued to tremble, and I glanced back up the pyramid. The Eagle Warriors were heading our way.

We found the stone-lined trail and stuck to it for a little while. Then Tessa pulled me off to the right and into the brushy growth there. He pushed me flat and dropped down beside me.

Bugs swarmed around us and settled. Birds gave cries of alert, but the sounds spread so far that it would not pinpoint our location. The ground shook again, and I heard the volcano rumbling with another eruption. I hoped the Priestess got that under control.

The men came closer and passed a few yards away. We remained still, and I let Tessa decide on when to move. I trusted his instincts, both the fae and the cat ones, even when he couldn't access the power.

"Into the jungle," he said and stood. I scrambled up to my feet beside him. He stared into my face, as somber and serious as I have ever seen him. "I am never taking a vacation with you again."

"Like this is my fault! We're blaming my sisters."

"True. But, in case of any future vacations, I'll err on the side of caution. It's not as though strange things don't happen around you at other times. Even the fae have noted that problem."

I couldn't argue with reality.

We headed into the shadowed jungle, neither of us speaking now. I had to focus on what we did now, and it wasn't easy. All I could see was that toomi blade in the warrior's hand. I didn't think Tessa understood. He would not have recognized that kind of knife and what it meant.

The shaking of the ground helped because each time, the island's animals cried out in agitation. The enemy would not track us with any ease.

Tessa soon realized that I wasn't paying enough attention. His worried look, and another vicious shake of the world, brought me back to my senses.

We could hear the Eagle Warriors. I didn't want to be the reason Tessa got caught. The Priestess would not be happy about our escape.

We had a problem, though. A lot of problems, but one that I noted just a moment too late. We'd rushed in under a pack of monkeys and birds. They screamed in surprise -- but another large quake shook the area.

Tessa pulled me to the side of a cycad with the tall, bushy leaves protecting us just as the men appeared. One started forward, but the capuchin monkeys protested, including shaking limbs and tossing fruit. The man backed away in haste. The ground shook once more. Every creature in the area screamed again.

I heard the Warriors speaking about the volcano. They hurried on, no doubt believing that the monkeys would have protested our presence.

Something with power must have been on our side. The quakes and the jungle creatures' behavior were nothing Tessa, or I could have easily managed, even with fae magic.

The men disappeared out of the area. We didn't dare stay, though. I heard another sound, and so did Tessa.

"Damn. The Priestess already sent out the jaguars!" I looked around in frantic haste. "We need to take to the trees and see if we can get clear of them."

"That doesn't seem likely," Tessa mumbled. He glanced upward. "Not here. Our friends have been cooperative, but they wouldn't like us invading their home with the big cats after us."

"True." We started away, and I remained aware this time. I could sometimes see a plume of ash shooting up into the air -- the volcano was far from done. "I wonder if anyone can detect the volcanic activity. The earthquakes, if nothing else --"

"I've seen reports about registering quakes out in the ocean and people having no idea where they originated," Tessa replied. "I don't think the fae would even notice -- though maybe we'll get lucky in this case. Our people will look for anything unusual and might stumble on this. You were right about the island being encased in a powerful shield. Something this magical should have drawn notice before now, but the protection must transmit a vision of nothing but ocean."

"I suspected something like that," I agreed. My knee ached, and I felt bruises growing where I'd fallen on the pyramid. "They were about to decapitate me."

Tessa stopped and looked at me with a sudden shock. "That odd blade --"

"An ancient Inca device. But the quake hit. And it hit again a few minutes ago when they almost captured us. Tessa, I think we have a powerful ally here."

"I've sensed a power in the temple."

"I wondered."

We said nothing for a while, listening as the sounds of large angry cats grew closer.

"That's insane," Tessa admitted with a shake of his head. "It would mean that you and I are here because something powerful wants our help."

"It could be chance," I replied, though I had stopped believing random circumstances about the time I joined up with the fae. "Or Karma. I don't think that anything could have manipulated my sisters without us realizing it. The whole 'vacation' idea has to be theirs."

"So maybe it just took notice once we were in the air."

"Or when Dagon decided to play games."

Tessa nodded and looked relieved. "Yes. I suspect the Priestess has something trapped in the temple. That would be our ally. And no, we can't try to get it free -- not until we have our powers back and a lot of fae with us."

I hoped that was going to happen soon. "We better get up into the trees."

"Cats can climb, you know."

"We will make our way through the canopy using the liana vines," I said, tapping one of the massive, ropy plants at the side of a trunk. "They'll lose our scent."

He looked up. "You want me to play Tarzan."

"It's more likely to be more George of the Jungle, but yeah. Unless you have a better kitty-inspired idea?"

"I would go for a good-sized stream -- but I've seen none, so I think the trees are our best plan. They don't look too difficult to climb."

"Watch out for snakes. I haven't spotted any yet, but that doesn't mean they aren't around. And spiders. And --"

"I get the idea."

Not far away, we found a bent palm reaching high enough

to get into the canopy. I'd climbed such trees before, and I had little trouble heading upward, though I felt out of practice. Tessa followed, slowly at first, but he got the idea.

The tree stood close enough to another, so we had little trouble swinging out onto another branch. Then we went on to the next, smaller tree. The branches swayed, but we moved onward. The cats drew closer, which helped in one way -- their presence scared off all the smaller animals, making a ruckus that covered our own noise.

We'd made it farther than I had expected -- at least ten trees before the Jaguar Warriors and their cat companions came too close, and we dared not move. I hoped we had enough cover where we were, and I still looked around, hoping for a quick escape, though I suspected that would not happen.

The jaguars had our scent, and getting up higher was not far enough away. We stayed still, but before long, they spotted us.

"Down," one man ordered. "Down, or we cut the tree down, and that won't make us any happier."

I looked at Tessa.

"Start thinking up a good wish," he whispered. "I suspect you won't get another chance."

Tessa went down first, but I followed. We faced the men and the jaguars -- and the cats were the real danger. The two men fought to hold them back as they growled, ears flattened. The reaction might be to Tessa and that essence of cat that was part of him.

"Tessa, get back," I ordered. "I don't think --"

One jaguar broke free and went for Tessa, who darted for

the nearest tree trunk and climbed. The second cat would soon follow or go for me. I had to do something drastic and fast.

I wanted to call in help, but my friends might not arrive soon enough, even if I got past the shield. The second jaguar strained the leash to get to me. Either I did something fast, or else I'd lose Tessa. It had to be something that wouldn't kill me by trying to alter too much. Something --

"I wish the local jaguars no longer hunted or killed people!"

Then I went down on my knees, the world going black and with no idea if I'd done that well or not. I had no sense of time. Tessa and I could die at any moment.

I could almost hear voices and knew that time had passed. A hand rested on my shoulder, which I recognized as Tessa's, before I looked up and blinked.

"Damn well done, Lord Summerfield," he said with a bow of his head.

"Tessa?" I asked, confused.

He knelt, his face pale. I supposed he thought he had been about to go kitten in the next couple of minutes.

"You spoke English," he told me with a slight smile. "They think you used some great spell to tame the jaguars -- which you did."

"I wanted to call the others in."

"That wish might not have gotten out of the shield. Will you be okay?"

"Pounding headache, of course. I suppose we'll walk back soon."

"Soon," he agreed. "But they are wary of you now."

I looked around without everything blurring. The big cats

sat placidly at the Jaguar Warriors' feet, and the men looked unsettled.

Time to create the start of a power base, I realized.

"I could have sent them against you rather than tame the jaguars," I said as I stood, keeping my hand to Tessa's shoulder, so I didn't fall flat on my face and ruin the show. "But we are not enemies of your people. Remember that when you get back."

Tessa rose as well. He had a claw mark down his left leg, and I tore some cloth from his ragged tunic and made a bandage to at least slow the bleeding. My knee ached to distraction, almost taking my attention from the headache. I wondered how much I could trust these men who escorted us back with one ahead and two behind. I had frightened them, and scared people sometimes did odd things.

CHAPTER 14

We had run so far from the city that we hiked two or more hours back with our unhappy guards. The jaguars had fun, rolling in the dirt, chasing hummingbirds, and pretty much acting like house cats. I'm sure that would please everyone.

We rested at a bench. Otherwise, our captors would have been carrying me since Tessa could barely walk, and I suspected the Jaguar Warriors feared to touch me. Apparently, cute, playful jaguars unsettled them.

We even stopped at the tambo where I had first seen the mosaic that so bothered me. It did not look better today. We had found too many odd things going on here, and I still couldn't sort it out.

I also couldn't see how to get free of this mess. This was not the way we wanted to live the rest of our lives.

The guards ordered us up, and we didn't argue. Tessa said nothing at all. He walked with a hand on my shoulder, but that wasn't to keep to his feet. His leg bled a bit, and he limped, but I could tell he worried more about me than himself. We were heading back to trouble. I had just used powerful magic, and the Priestess was going to want that power. I couldn't give it to her. Wish for her to have it? And would that make me any less dead? Either giving it to her would kill me, or else I would die at her hands once she had what she wanted.

I still believed that Brandis, Kala, and the others were our best chance at getting out of here. They wouldn't give up looking for the lost Totem for the Cat Clan. Even if Tessa had died, he would have been reborn as a kitten, and they'd search all the world for him.

The big cats continued to play. I thought the monkeys would stay safe from them, being human-like. Sometimes I saw their ears go up and heads turn. They had to hunt to eat. Others would not feed them out of kindness, so it would be best if they fended for themselves. I wondered how many of the jaguars there were on the island. I had limited the wish to this location. Without the location limitation, the wish would have spread over the South American continent -- and to jaguars around the world in zoos. It would have killed me.

I'd saved us. The headache would ease. I had to walk back to the city and deal with the Priestess. I remembered seeing the toomi blade and shuddered. How could I escape that fate this time?

The ground shook again. The volcano grumbled and went silent. I gave a sigh of relief, and I thought the guards did as well.

The jaguars flanked Tessa and me. I didn't think that would help, either. We came down the hillside into the valley, and I could hear sounds of surprise and worry.

We found problems in the city. People shouted, and I saw the smoke of fires in various spots where walls had fallen during the quakes. A group from the city had gathered at the pyramid's base, shouting with annoyance and worry. I couldn't make out what they said even when we hurried past them. Eagle Warriors had lined the area and held the others back.

We went up the ramps. I didn't see the Priestess at first, but it turned out that she had been sitting on the ramp.

That tired and weak? Keeping the volcano in hand must be taxing. She and her priests -- who weren't as powerful as her -- must have thrown everything they could at it. The air almost glowed with the spells.

Too much trouble. I didn't want the volcano to let loose a wave of destruction, but I couldn't give magic to this woman, either. Could I stop the eruption?

"If I wished the volcano --"

"Only if you have no other choice," Tessa said and looked at me, worry narrowing his eyes. "You wouldn't survive it so soon after the last wish, and I doubt it would work, anyway. I would rather have you alive to help us."

I didn't argue.

As Tessa and I climbed back up the pyramid, I realized that I found the building far less interesting the more time I spent climbing it. Up and up, my leg hurting and Tessa limping worse than me.

The jaguars darted up and down the ramp, running and playing. I found it amusing. The Priestess, I could tell, looked more appalled than amused or afraid. A Jaguar Warrior hurried up ahead of us -- not a problem as slow as Tessa and I moved. He knelt and said something fast to the woman. Her head came up, and she focused on me with a look of curiosity.

We took the last few steps as she stood.

"What have you done to my jaguars?" she asked. Not demanded.

"I have made certain they won't hurt another human." I had to fight not to sway as a wave of exhaustion hit me again. "And no, I cannot undo it."

"Cannot or will not?"

"Cannot," I replied, which was at least accurate for the moment. If I had tried to wish it, I knew I would not survive to get that far. She must have believed me, but it didn't help our cause.

Agitation continued at the base of the temple. The Priestess sent a priest and many of her Eagle Warriors down with instructions that directed people to various helpful jobs. I could see that the warriors were eager to help in the city. Even the Jaguar Warriors, with their odd new companions, headed off to help. The Priestess gave orders to her priests as well, but they headed back up to the temple to make sure that the building stayed intact. This was not her first earthquake, though, from the way the locals reacted, it could not happen often.

That made me remember that she might be more akin to Tessa in age than to me. Could I use that somehow? Was there anything I could do to dissuade her from killing us? We needed time, that was all. The others would find us. Soon.

A sudden scream of anger came from the area of the huts drew all our attention. The slaves, both men and women, rushed out in a mass, and they had made weapons and shields. In the front of the pack, they were led by --

My five sisters.

I wasn't even surprised. Why hadn't I asked what they'd been doing lately? I had left the Flowers on their own for several days. Of course, they'd come up with something ...

dramatic.

The group rushed to the pyramid, fought their way past the too few startled soldiers, and kept heading to reach Tessa and me. I tried to wave them away, but when had my sisters ever listened to me? The slaves were few, but they were forceful in their rush up the stairs. I think they might have planned to grab the Priestess. My sisters were trying to reach Tessa and me, though. I don't know what we'd do once we got free, but I decided not to argue. I just hoped --

We felt the ground shake with a stronger tremor. The Priestess gave a shout and directed power to settle the land again, but the quake had sent many of the slaves tumbling. My sisters were back on their feet first and rushing up the last ramp.

Some of the Eagle Warriors had seen the trouble and rushed back. They had no problem getting everyone hemmed in at my left, though they remained wary of the weapons. Rose shouted orders, and the slaves scattered. There would be more trouble for them if they didn't get a foothold into the power structure during this disaster. I wished them well, but it would not help Tessa and me -- or my sisters.

The Priestess turned to us, her eyes blazing. "I offer you one last chance to give me your power."

"No," I said. Tessa just met her stare with a glare of his own.

"The great god Quetzalcoatl, whose benevolent name is Kukulcán, had given you a chance to live in his radiances and to bask before his light. I could behead you, but I have seen that you never use your power against others. You help improve the crops. So, for now ... for now, you will bow down into the dirt and grovel with the lowest of the low, never to receive the joys of being one of the chosen." Her lips curled back into a caricature of a smile. I could tell we had decided in a way that pleased her. "You have doomed yourself to live forever in drudgery, remaining in this place for the rest of your lives, and always thinking about what you might have been instead."

I grinned. Tessa looked at me as though I had gone insane. The Priestess's stare wasn't much better.

"If we are to stay here for the rest of our lives, Tessa, I'd say our journey is over."

Tessa's fear and rage turned to shock. A slight breeze blew out of nowhere, and macaws that had been roosting on the pyramid took to the air with shouts of surprise. I felt the magic return -- and so did the Priestess who backed away from Tessa in haste. Tessa spun, literally howling as he changed into a cat --

The Priestess screamed in alarm. Soldiers either scattered or starred in shock, unmoving.

"Tessa!" I shouted in frustration as he charged a couple priests, sending them stumbling backward. "Stop that and call the others in first!"

He looked back at me with a little growl but changed again.

"Yes, bring our friends in for this fun!" Tessa lifted his hand and gave a wave of magic. What he did was showy on purpose. The spear of bright blue light shot straight up like a beacon, casting odd shadows everywhere. I saw the beacon hit the shield, pause, and push through in a sparkle of stars that destroyed a large section of the magic that had kept us hidden.

A heartbeat later, Brandis appeared.

"What the hell is going on!" he demanded. Then he saw someone with a spear charging toward me. He waved his hand and broke the weapon in half, and sent the man backward to land on his ass. "Don't do that! Summerfield --"

His face went pale, and he stared past me. I turned.

My sisters. I had forgotten them in that moment of inspiration.

Rose stared at me and shook her head. "Well damn, Sunflower! Why didn't you say you were dealing with the fae? Everything makes so much more sense now!"

CHAPTER 15

I stared at Rose for a moment too long, wondering if this was some sort of trick. All the work I'd done to keep my second life quiet, and --

"We have problems," Tessa shouted. "Look out!"

The Priestess had gotten over her shock. The bolt of an angry blue spell she sent at Brandis and I would have destroyed us, but Tessa and Brandis swept it away. We were in an actual battle, against both magic and spears.

More of my clan arrived in a blast of light and power. Fae spread out in sets of double squares as soon as they saw the trouble. Tessa -- and with him, Kala -- focused on the Priestess. She looked more appalled than afraid. The Priestess and two of her priests retreated up the ramp, trying to reach the temple. With each step closer, she appeared to grow more powerful.

"We can't take her here!" I said to Brandis. "I don't want to lose anyone. Let's regroup!"

Brandis gave a quick nod of agreement. I think he had contact with Kala. They both directed us as we fought our way down the pyramid to better cover. My sisters took instructions well, though even they looked stunned. That might have been because of Tessa, who kept charging back and forth in cat form. He had a lot of pent up energy and frustration.

"Tessa, I see, is not happy," Kala said. She moved to help keep a shield around us and directed others as the Cat Clan Warlord. "What the hell happened, Summerfield?"

"Let's wait until I can tell everyone about my stupidity, rather than spreading it out," I suggested. "I don't want to have to retell the story several times."

She made an amused sound. "This is an odd place," she said, looking around.

"Yeah, we noticed."

"And you have not been well," she added and took my arm. Then her face went hard. "Tell me, Lord Summerfield, that is not a scar from a whip on the side of your neck."

Oh, hell. That mark would be from the quirt where the Overseer had struck me a few times. I had forgotten. If the others grew enraged, there was no telling what they might do. I wanted to handle this well.

"Calm, Kala. We have many people to free and rights to wrong."

"There will be an accounting for this," she replied, which sounded far too much like an oath to me.

I took hold of her arm, and she looked at me, eyes narrowed.

"Not now, Kala. We have problems. These people have power. We need to make certain everyone they've held captive for so long gets free of them without us making matters worse."

"Right," she said, and took a deeper breath and calmed. Good, because she had looked ready to flatten everything.

As the magical battle grew fierce, the Eagle and Jaguar

Warriors retreated out of the way, and anyone without magic had gone to cover. The Priestess and her close followers seemed matched with the fae in magic.

The entire group oathed to me had arrived, except for Arinith. I would rather he didn't show up unless we absolutely needed him. The Fae prince was a problem when he came to our realm.

I looked up. Yes, those were clouds rolling in. We were in for some foul weather. Dagon had gotten in on the game.

The bottom of the pyramid proved no safer than the top. A lightning strike came close enough that even this powerful of a shield took damage from the attack. A sliver of dark power found me, and I went to my knees.

York grabbed me as we moved away. I didn't like to see him caught up in battle, being the Dragon Clan Bard. He got me moving, though. Kala was looking around, frantic, and then pointed to a building across from us. The place looked small, lined with cloth and pillows. It might be a shop, I thought.

"There," she yelled and directed the others. Brandis held the rear for our group, which included my sisters. "Clear that building, and we can shield it --"

"Don't hurt them," I ordered, catching hold of her arm. "Just the priesthood has any power."

"Ah. And damned odd magic, too." Kala looked annoyed. "I don't know how you find trouble like this, Summerfield."

"I could blame it on all of you," I replied and won a raised eyebrow. "But then I'd have to come up with a reason that I fell in with the fae in the first place. How do we get across to the building?"

Brandis had joined us. So did Tessa, though he panted, even in fae form. His leg bled worse, but I didn't think he noticed.

"A triple shield," Brandis decided as others formed a square around us. He frowned. "They seem to have a lot of power."

"I see the priests go into the temple at the top of the pyramid," Kala said with a wave of her hand. "I suspect they are replenishing their magic."

"Are they?" Brandis looked up at the building and frowned. "That will be a problem for us. Ready, Kala?"

"Yes," she said.

"Tessa?" he asked.

"I'm ready."

York had used a spell to help with Tessa's leg, but though the injury remained. They were trying to conserve power.

I turned to my sisters, who, despite knowing about fae, appeared shocked by all the activity. "Do whatever they say. Kala, Brandis --"

"Yes, yes," Kala said. "Keep them safe. Get them out. The usual."

Tessa laughed. He patted Kala on the shoulder. "We have a lot to set right here."

"Good." She smiled.

And that was why they were my people. I could trust them to help where they could.

We made our way across the courtyard to the building. Kala remained at the lead and Brandis at the back, and two squares moved in around us. Tessa kept with me in the middle, and the amount of magic they used created so bright a glow that it hurt to look beyond it. We still felt the brunt of the attack from above.

Kala reached the door and shoved aside the cloth covering. Someone inside screamed. Kala rushed in, but I saw how she brushed her hand over the wall. The shield she'd carried now spread out over the small building.

Three locals cowered into the corner. York moved to stand by them, an effective enough guard since they had no weapons. The rest of us crowded in. Tessa added his shield to Kala's, and Brandis merged his magic as well. Even the interior glowed.

We had a safe spot for the moment, but we were not free. And if the Priestess had any kind of insight into my character - - and I suspected she did -- she would turn her attack on someone unprotected.

"We need to protect the slaves," I said to Kala.

"Slaves. Here. I will not like this place much, Summerfield."

"You aren't alone," I admitted, even while I still wanted to study everything. "The slaves live in that area between the pyramid and the swamp. They had started a rebellion -- I'm sure my sisters were behind it -- but there are children. The Priestess will go for them, knowing I will do whatever I can to protect them. She understands me at least that well."

"I'll take a couple of our people and get to them," Brandis said. I wasn't sure I wanted Brandis where I couldn't see him, but it was for the best. "It's a good idea since I need to feel out more of that pyramid. It's the center of their power. We need to know how to cut them off from it, or we'll face a damned long siege on both sides. No, Tessa. You stay and rest a bit. You look little better than Lord Summerfield."

Tessa started to protest but stopped and bowed his head.

Tessa and I went to the back of the room and found places to sit opposite the two women and a man who had calmed since no one had attacked him. Perhaps I should talk to them, but I just didn't have the energy to pull up another language.

I let my people take over. I trusted the fae to do what they could, and they didn't need me to point out that they shouldn't hurt anyone who didn't fight them.

Tessa gave me a wry grin.

"Good catch on how to break the oath, Summerfield," he admitted with a bow of his head. "I was so irate I didn't even see the little loophole."

"This mess is going to be harder to clean up than I thought, though," I replied.

"We can get you out of here," he said. "I would suggest it, but I know you wouldn't agree."

"You're right. I may not be much help, but I can't walk away from here. I wish I --"

He threw himself over the top of me. I hit my head on the wall.

"Yeah," I said. "Thanks for the reminder."

Tessa pulled himself back to sit up again. Then I noticed that my sisters had settled close by. Rose looked amused but also shocked.

"He can't be trusted," Tessa explained to them. "We're having a hellish time breaking him of that habit."

"I feel like a pet puppy," I complained.

Rose, Carnation, and Lily laughed. Not the fae, though. They looked a bit appalled. Sometimes they still didn't see how to deal with me.

"You turned into a cat," Aster said as she waved a hand toward Tessa. "From all I've learned about the fae, that's not very common."

"Why do you know anything about them?" I asked, surprised again.

Violet leaned forward this time and shook her head in disbelief. "Sunflower, when did you forget that we have the same parents?"

I looked at her, startled again. "You're right."

"Up to a certain point in our lives, we all had much the same education -- and adventures. Then the three of you went off on a quest for enlightenment. We used to travel around the states, you know. Met some wonderful, interesting people, including quite a few modern shamans. We knew about the fae, but we had no contact with them until after you and the parents left. A couple from the Wolf Clan would show up at the old family farm if any of us stopped by there. I did not think there were so many in our realm."

She said the last to Tessa with a still elegant eyebrow raised.

"Wars, refuge, exile," I offered. "And I just fell in with them."

"They call you Lord Summerfield," Carnation added.

"They do." I tried to come up with a way to explain it.

"I am the Cat Clan Totem," Tessa explained. "That means I am a shape-changer. Kala is our Warlord. Brandis, who went to help the slaves, is the Dragon Clan Warlord. In a normal situation, we would not mix. However, we also serve Summerfield in a special clan, created for those of us here in your realm."

"You know this all sounds insane," Aster admitted.

"Yes, it does. Try living it," I replied.

"This is as close as I care to get."

"You are wiser than I am," I said. I rubbed at the sore spot on the back of my head where I'd hit the wall. Tessa did not look contrite.

York settled next to me. The locals remained calm since we didn't threaten them. I saw Kala hanging close to them, though. The fae took nothing for granted.

"Lord Summerfield, sir," York said with a half-hidden grin and deep bow of his head. "May I suggest, your Lordship, that you *never take another vacation.* If you try to propose such a thing, or if we find you have wandered off by yourself, we will not be responsible for what we do."

Coming from York, that was quite a statement. I grinned. "Did Kala send you to tell me that one?"

"Yes," he admitted and then sighed dramatically. "You know, I still have trouble with the idea that a Cat Clan member can tell me to do anything at all."

"And just this poor Cat Clan totem, caught amid that madness with humans and Dragon Clan," Tessa added. "Summerfield, any clue what we're going to do now?"

"Not yet," I replied, more serious. "We have the entire clan here? Vane --"

"Over there," York nodded to the right. Vane stood close by a window, staring out at the temple. "We didn't dare leave him behind. He has given his word that he will stay calm and not shape change. It's a test for him."

"Keep him safe. I don't think any of us want to go through hatching another dragon egg," Tessa said. Lily looked at him, her eyes gone wide. "Yes, Vane is the Dragon Clan totem and a dragon in his other shape. But he's young -- just returned to the world after a disastrous battle where his ancient form died."

Lily nodded. I thought I could see a bit of how I must have looked in that blinking, deer-in-the-headlights look she gave us. The other Flowers were not any better. Even though they may have met a few fae, that was not the same as falling into an adventure with them.

I almost said you get used to it, but that would be a lie. You just learned to live with it after a while.

The battle had died down. My fae began talking about levels of power and how to do the most damage without killing anyone. I saw how Lily and Carnation both caught that line and looked surprised and pleased.

We had quiet, though I could hear men yelling somewhere else in the city. The ground shook once more with a quick jolt and sway of the walls. Then the earth settled again, and I heard no sound of more trouble from the volcano. I rested, glad that most of the problem was now out of my hands. The relief almost overcame the worry about getting *my* people into this mess.

After a while, Kala came over and settled on the floor by Tessa and me. She patted the Cat Clan Totem on the arm. I could imagine how worried she must have been.

"We cannot breach their hold on the pyramid, Summerfield," Kala explained. She pushed back her hair in a gesture of annoyance and worry. "Whatever is giving them power seems inexhaustible. We cannot find how to circumvent it."

"Can we seal them off instead?" Tessa asked. He looked restless.

"For a short time, perhaps," she said with a glance to the window. We could barely see the pyramid through the glow of the shields. "But they'd continue to access their power and pound their way out before too long."

Tessa nodded. He turned to me. "Maybe the best thing we can do is get everyone but the priesthood off of the island, seal the place off, and figure out how to deal with them later. The Queen might have an idea."

I glanced back at the people whose shop we had invaded. They didn't look happy, and I couldn't blame them. We had put them in danger. Could we take them out? They had no skills, language, or link of any kind with the outside world, a place where even magic was not real.

"What do we do with them?" I asked, drawing both Kala and Tessa's attention. "It's not like we can just move all these people into some apartment house in the middle of a city and turn them loose."

"Hell. Good point," Kala replied. She looked at the strangers as well and gave them a polite nod, though I doubt they appreciated her attempt to look friendly. "How do you find these messes, Summerfield?"

"It's a gift," I said.

"Return it," Tessa mumbled.

And we laughed again. Damn, that felt good. I had to believe that nothing could be so terrible that we couldn't figure it out.

CHAPTER 16

Vane crossed the room and sat by us. He looked nervous, and the others kept an eye on him. When I started to say something, Vane lifted a hand and stared towards the door, his eyes wide and unblinking. We could see the pyramid's base from here through the waves of light that comprised the shield. He watched for a few heartbeats and then shook his head.

"What do they have there?" he asked with a frown. He sounded too mature, which I wasn't sure I liked. Having a teenage, shape-shifting dragon had been remarkable. I enjoyed being around the kid.

I remembered something that was not from my past but rather from the Dragon Clan Key I had worn for a while. The memory showed me the older Vane giving his life to save those around him. He had hadn't known if his egg would survive. He'd been noble, and I knew I would respect that Vane ... but I didn't want him to grow up yet.

I tried to bury that self-centered feeling. The Dragon Clan needed the full power of their Totem back. I just wanted my friend to enjoy life. Vane did, especially if we kept him in pizza.

We had not answered his question, but Kala patted him on the arm. "We'll figure it out, Vane. You realize you don't have to be here, right? I think we can get you back home."

"I know," he said, and then he grinned. "But you guys have all the fun."

"Fun." Tessa looked around.

Vane laughed. It was a pleasant sound to hear, and it cheered everyone again.

Except for the shop owners. They represented other problems, and I realized I was going to have to come up with answers. They kept quiet for the moment, though.

The ground shook.

Walls moved with a spattering of dust and small debris while the ceiling cracked.

"Out!" Tessa shouted. He threw magic out the door and formed a shield that glowed with a white light beyond the opening. The others held to the one around the building, but it would not hold up for long.

We rushed outside. The quake, which had been short-lived, seemed to be over --

No. It started again as the stone pavement beneath our feet bounced and rolled. I went to my knees and looked up at the pyramid. Yes, the Priestess waved her arm, and the quake moved with it.

"Attack on us," Tessa said and grabbed my arm. He had trouble enough with the shield, so Vane took hold of me. "Localized. We try to head inside, and she'll bring down the building."

"Go to the pyramid?" I asked.

"That would be what she wants," Kala replied with more than her usual glare. "I think she could trap us there. Ah. Brandis."

I looked up and found Brandis and a group of about thirty slaves. The priests standing atop the pyramid focused on them, but those men held less powerful magic than the Priestess. Brandis kept his companions safe behind his shield.

I feared the ground was going to open up and bury us.

"We don't dare stay in one place." I looked around, frantic for an answer. "Not inside."

"We could run for the fields, but I doubt we'd get that far," Tessa said. He looked pale, and his hands trembled. We needed to move out of range so he and the others could recover. "But we might as well try. We can take this group to safety, at least."

"Let's go. I don't know how we're going to escape from the island."

"We'll find a way," Tessa replied. We were already moving toward a path that was not next to the pyramid.

However, when we neared the stairs leading out of the valley, the entire cliff began to shake, and boulders rolled down. We backed away, but the fae prepared to stand their ground, at least where they could stand at all. We were mostly out in the open, though, and the fae had too many people to protect. This was not going well.

Four of the Summerfield Clan formed into a square with the humans, including me, in the middle. The next group created another four-cornered box around the first one, which would help power the magic. Vane stood at the center of our power. He held his place as we moved, his eyes narrowed in concentration.

I knew we couldn't hold back the Priestess for long.

"What do we do?" I asked, wincing as more stone crashed

downward and bounced away. Once the magic broke, those boulders would come through.

"She's getting weaker," Tessa replied. He panted, but his hands moved, and he added his power to the protective shell. "We need to get everyone to some cover. Where?"

With a frantic glance around, I spotted a single building that might work. "I think our best chance to find safety is to head for the Sapa Inca," I said. I glanced at the shopkeepers who had looked up at the name.

"What is this Inca?" Kala asked from her point in the nearest square protecting us. We inched our way from the cliff, but there would be no sign of where we intended to go yet.

"The last true ruler of the Inca Empire," I explained in a rush. "Pizarro executed him in 1533. The Catholic Priests did their best to destroy all the mummies because the Inca celebrated ancestor worship, but this one survived. I suspect the Spanish intended to ship Atahualpa's mummy to Europe as another piece of treasure, but he ended up here. The locals reverence him. That monumental building is his, and he has his own guards."

"The Jaguar Warriors dislike us since Summerfield wished their jaguars tame," Tessa warned the others. "But at least they don't have magic."

"The Priestess appears to be more Aztec than Incan," I said. "I can't be sure she'll care about the Sapa Inca."

"I suspect the Priestess has never had a serious opponent before, Summerfield. If she has ruled for hundreds of years, she may have lost all ability to reason well. We are a threat to everything she uses to rule."

"I sense the desperation in her power," York added. We all winced as more boulders fell down the cliff. "She's already on edge."

"Can we make it to the jungle instead?"

"No," Tessa replied, and the others agreed. "She's doing something different."

I could see it. A glow covered the top of the pyramid and then grew brighter with a flickering flame. I could feel the power. That deadly spell would engulf the shield that the fae had put around us. It would wear our magic away --

"To the Sapa Inca," I ordered. I didn't see where we had any choice unless we tried to get back to take her stronghold. I wasn't suicidal.

The slaves didn't argue and moved with us, too used to obeying commands, though that helped. Some held children. My sisters walked among them and urged them on whenever someone cried out in fear. The fireball grew so large it cast extra shadows across the land as if the Priestess had created a second sun to cleanse the city. I hoped that everyone else kept clear of them. At least the attacks kept focused on my group.

Tessa stayed with me. He looked back and shook his head, but I didn't turn to see. We took the main road downward, heading for the large square and the ornate tomb. I thought the Priestess would attack soon, but we reached the building's entrance, even with the ground shaking again.

I saw the shadows moving just as the last of the fae stepped inside. The fireball was coming for us!

Brandis yelled something. The others fell out of their squares and then reformed as best they could within the small entry hall. The slaves and my sister moved past, rushing for better cover. Tessa grabbed my arm and dragged me along. I looked back to see that the two squares had created such a massive shield that it almost blocked out the glow of the fireball. Now that everyone was inside, the fae backed away from the opening, though they still held to their squares. The light swirled beyond the building like a thing alive and trying to get in to devour us. She couldn't hold it much longer, could she? I didn't know. I turned to ask Tessa --

People yelled in surprise and fear as a spear grazed along the side of my arm.

Soldiers lined the upper-level gallery, standing shoulder-to-shoulder with the statues of their gods by the entrance.

The Priestess had driven us into a trap.

"Oh hell!"

Tessa, who was not part of the squares, used his magic and tried to sweep the soldiers off of the higher level. He took a few down, but someone's spear caught him in the shoulder. He fell with a grunt of pain and surprise.

Two people on the outer square started to fall, but others held them in place. Once that shield gave way, we would all perish. Even the soldiers, though I doubted telling them so that would change their attitudes. They had the looks of fanatics.

And I was helpless to stop any of this.

Or maybe not.

"I wish that fire spell would die!"

I went straight down to my knees with a bone-jarring drop. The wish proved more manageable to handle against magic than jaguars, though I gasped for breath and saw nothing but flashes of light until I blinked a few times. The spell had disappeared. As the squares broke up, the fae fought the soldiers, who began running out of spears. That battle did not take long, and the surviving Jaguar Warriors retreated along the gallery, heading toward the exit.

York arrived to help with Tessa. He pulled out the spear; the wound bled, but the Bard's magic stemmed that flow.

The trap had not killed us after all.

I was just about to say so when the ground gave a violent shake. I didn't even have time to curse before the walls and ceiling cracked, ready to collapse. Something hit me on the side of the head...

"She is a persistent bitch. I'll give her that," Kala growled from somewhere close by.

The Cat Clan Warlord did not sound happy, and I heard others grunt agreement. Someone hushed an unhappy child.

"Summerfield?" Brandis said as I moved.

"We survived again?" I asked, uncertain if I wanted the truth.

"Oh yes. The Priestess didn't have enough power left to pull the entire building down on us," Tessa replied with a bit of a snarl in his voice. "Unfortunately, she will replenish her magic before too long."

I sat up. I felt battered, and my head hurt to distraction. We had a few glowing lights floating around the interior of the ruined hall. I could see considerable damage to the room where I had knelt before the Sapa Inca, though I thought the area around him looked clear. The slaves, and even the shopkeepers, had gathered in a huddle in that location. Paul hovered between both groups, looking uncertain and half-wild again. The fae and my sisters stayed closer to me.

"Soldiers?" I asked.

Tessa shook his head. "They were all along the wall by the door when the quake pulled that section down. I don't think we could have saved them even if we had tried. We did not, Summerfield, since we had enough to keep the others from being buried."

"We were lucky because all of us were heading away from the door," Brandis added. "That gave the fae a smaller area to protect. Now, do you want the good news, Summerfield?"

"Good news? There is such a thing in this place?" I asked.

"A little. We included a touch of unique magic to the shield that blends in better. All that the woman should see is the dying flickers of our magic and fallen stones. We don't believe she knows we're alive in here."

"Ah! How long can we stay?"

"Not long," Tessa admitted. "But at least this time, we should have some surprise."

"And we have to go for the pyramid once we are free," Brandis decided. Kala gave an emphatic nod. "Until we cut her, and the rest of the priesthood, away from that power source, we don't have a chance."

"Unless we retreat," I said. "Get out and leave this island --"

Tessa shook his head. "Can't let you do that, Summerfield. This land, with its slavery and other evils, represents a wrong in your realm. You -- and the fae by association -- are obligated to fix the problem. If you don't, it's going to weaken your power and then ours. So much so that we might not have the magic to find the place again. It would work like an open wound, weakening us all."

"This is getting to be bothersome."

Tessa laughed in agreement.

"What do we do?" I asked.

"Rest. We're able to use a minimum amount of power here," Tessa said. "Your sisters are taking care of the others. The slaves will remain here when we go."

I nodded and didn't ask what would happen to them if we failed. There was no sense in asking for more trouble and angst. We needed, instead, to prepare.

"How are we going to do this?" I asked.

CHAPTER 17

We'd had to work our way out of the rubble with slow and careful movements. The fae had removed the bodies of the dead so that any power they might have had bled away into the night. The physical debris of the ruin remained, and for that, my people dared not use more magic, except to make sure nothing more came down on us. My arms hurt, but I did my part in moving blocks. When we reached the blocked doorway, we rested, ready for more trouble.

"The Priestess used considerable magic to destroy this building, so I don't think she's going to feel the little that I laid down," Kala said. She looked worried, but no one felt any sign of trouble yet.

"Excellent work."

We rested. The Priestess might have drained her levels of power -- but how fast could she recharge?

My sisters sometimes watched me, and they must have been making some new assessments about who I'd become when they weren't looking. I'm sure they still thought I was crazy but in a novel and creative way.

We had all survived. I could see the ruined doorway ahead, with our opening high up on the wall of debris. I could see no light beyond the entrance. We had worked for hours, but I thought we must still be some time before the dawn.

Tessa pressed up beside me and looked out. He gave a quick nod and smile, wiping the dirt from his face.

"Two hours until light," he said. "Don't start without me."

"Tessa --"

"Do nothing stupid, Summerfield."

Then he squirmed out of the opening and disappeared into the night.

I held my breath, expecting to see a flash of light and to hear him yowl. Instead, I listened to his four feet rushing away.

Good, so far.

I slid down the small tunnel and sat with the rest of my companions. I was used to having Tessa at my side to translate for me, but maybe that was unfair to the others. We understood each other very well these days.

"Vane?" I said, looking at him. He stared at the opening.

"I'll be ready," he replied. He looked steady. Then he grinned with a mischievous glint in his dark eyes. "The sooner we fix this problem, the faster we can get home to have pizza, right?"

"Right," I said with a bright smile.

The others laughed. I saw a few nervous looks towards the opening. I thought they worried that the Priestess and her people would find us. Then I suspected something else in those anxious stares.

"You don't trust Tessa," I said aloud.

Brandis looked embarrassed.

Kala laughed. "Tessa is a cat, Summerfield. We just sent a

cat to help set up a dangerous and complex trap. You're not worried?"

"He does sometimes seem, well..."

"Cat-like," Kala supplied.

Aster arrived to talk and found a set of fae who tried not to giggle. That didn't appear to help her view of the future, though she sat down.

"Everything is okay?" Aster asked.

"Yes, it is," I said. "I think we'll have this settled soon. You realize we might not win, right? So far, the Priestess has fought off every bit of magic we've been able to pull together. We're going to try being tricky instead."

"They say she is not one of the fae," Aster said with a frown. "What is she then? A demon?"

"No," Brandis replied. "We've fought demons. She's human, but she's pulling power from something that is not human and is immensely powerful. I suspect she has a magic well of some sort in that pyramid. Once we 'cap' that source, she's going to be losing her magic. Then she'll just be a bad-tempered human. We've learned how to deal with those."

And he put a hand on my shoulder.

"When have I ever been bad-tempered!" I replied in shock.

"We don't have time for those tales right now," he replied.

The others laughed, and so did I. I don't know what Aster thought of the show, but I suspected Brandis had provided an answer that had won my sisters over. He had made us all human at that moment. Reachable.

"Whatever happens, you are going to have your hands full with those poor people," I said, nodding back toward the others. "We will do our best to get them off of this island, but I don't know what we'll do after we're clear of this place."

"I'm not sure they'll agree to leave," Aster replied, and then she lifted a hand. "Oh, they want out of slavery. However, for some, this has been their home for generations, you know. For others, they've been here so long they couldn't go back to their old lives, anyway."

I understood more of the problem we would face once we removed the priesthood from their power. The former slaves, the elite, the middle class, and whatever Warriors might remain must all learn to work with each other because I feared we couldn't move them out into the world.

"We'll do what we can," I said to her. "After we survive this mess."

Aster agreed as she leaned back. We fall felt exhausted. "I'm sorry for this trouble, Sunflower -- but we've all had a chance to do something extraordinary here."

"I should have realized when you had this sudden urge for a vacation that there was more at the heart of it. Someone wanted me here."

"None of us felt an outside force aimed at you, no matter what the source," Kala reminded me. "I worry about what else might have come into play."

"Yes," Vane agreed. "It is going to be an interesting future."

I looked at the Dragon Clan totem. "Why are you here? You took no oath to me, Vane, like the others."

"I told you," he said and smiled. "You people have all the fun. Should I be sitting in the Fontenelle Forest, waiting? Trying not to draw notice? With no pizza? Is that where you want me to be?"

"No," I replied.

"No," Brandis repeated. "You are coming back into yourself, Vane. It's good. But trust us still to know better than you, sometimes."

"I do," he replied with a bow of his head. "I want to survive since I'm finding life fascinating. Sometimes I see glimpses of my former life. I suspect I shouldn't say this, but I think it looked very boring."

I started to speak and stopped when I saw the looks on the faces of my other companions.

"You like it here, all of you," I said with a shake of my head. "It's more exciting."

"We had that war at the end," Brandis reminded me with a snarl. "That's not forgotten or forgiven. We will still deal with Gryn and Roan. However, we have found other reasons to stay with you, Summerfield."

"Those from the Cat Clan were here for a long time," Kala added. "But we were never became drawn into the society. That was Gryn's fault. I didn't know it could be this exciting, and yes, I am glad to take part in even this mess. This is a way to make amends. We turned our back on anything we could have done, and we snarled at humans and Dragon Clan both, as though they were the same thing. You are helping us win back our honor."

I had learned over the last year never to argue with the fae over their honor. I bowed my head and looked outside. The darkness remained silent except for the sound of insects and some small creature hurrying through the shadows. I'd heard no indication of trouble, so I had to assume that Tessa had made his way out of the danger zone.

"How are the rest of the Unholy Five doing?" I asked as I looked at Aster.

"Oh, you don't still call us that!" Aster said with a look of shock. "Flowers is bad enough!"

"Why shouldn't I? You still call me Sunflower. Are you going to stop?"

"I doubt it."

"Then get used to the title. How are they doing?"

"They're worried about their families, but they know everyone in Omaha will be all right. None of them have shown any reluctance to help here. I work in a hospital, and I'm used to some level of helping others. They're lawyers. They don't get to do this hands-on stuff so often. I suspect that might change once we're back home."

"Thanks, Aster."

She nodded and looked out the opening for a moment. "I hope Tessa is okay."

Then Aster crawled over the debris to join the others. I wished she'd stayed for a little longer. She had been a pleasant distraction.

We heard sounds outside. Brandis moved forward, his magic ready. Nothing happened, so the Priestess must still believe that we hadn't survived. There had been no more quakes or fireballs.

I had feared the two hours would drag on, but all too soon, I could see the faint hint of dawn. We began crawling out of the rubble. I could tell Brandis and Kala wanted me to stay behind. That would not happen, so they didn't even waste their breath.

The fae used a minuscule touch of magic to make certain we remained silent. Vane stuck with Brandis as the front of the group. He knew what to do when the time came, but his part in this still worried everyone.

We stayed in the darker shadows. I heard sounds in some buildings. Many of the locals must have remained awake and terrified through the long night. I wondered if any considered how the loss of the slave population put them in a very precarious position with the priesthood. That group wasn't going to do the labor in the fields.

Six of us, including Tessa, left the ruins to do this work. The others had orders to survive as best they could. I hoped they still found a way out if we failed.

Brandis and Vane located a place to take cover just as the sun broke over the horizon. As the light of dawn came up over the edge of the valley, several people took food to the lower level of the pyramid, which must have been their usual job. A handful of soldiers came down and carried the few baskets up. The priesthood had not shown themselves yet. We waited.

The dawn turned cloudy with the volcano a dull grayish color against the sky. The day would soon turn hot and humid. I felt a slight touch of Dagon there, but since the dream about the Inca and Aztec gods, he'd held back.

I heard the first yells of fear.

"Good," Brandis said with a feral grin. "That should get everyone in an uproar."

Even I couldn't watch without my heartbeat kicking up in dread. Dozens of jaguars rushed down the mountainside stairs that led into the valley. I saw them as a line of black with one golden cat amid them.

The cats yowled and howled, and if I hadn't trusted Tessa to keep them in hand, I would have expected a bloodbath, even after my wish. People ran screaming as they sought cover.

The six priests took their position at the top of the pyramid, while behind them came the Priestess. She had not put on her mask. Since she had destroyed the place that the Jaguar Warriors protected, the lack of the mask might have been a political move. The rush of the Jaguars could even look like retribution against her.

She shouted, and the priests lifted their hands and prepared as the cats raced up the ramps towards them.

They were not ready for us, though.

Brandis patted Vane on the arm and went past, firing enough magic into the air that I thought he wouldn't need the help of the others. Two of the priests fell, rolling down the ramp and not getting back up. Tessa leapt over one and kept going, while the Priestess raised a shield with a wave of her hand.

Perfect. While the Priestess remained within that magical wall, there was little she could do against us.

Vane watched the battle for a moment and then nodded. "I must go. Be careful, Lord Summerfield."

"You, as well."

He smiled and walked back to a broader opening before he shifted into his dragon form. He had grown since the last time I'd seen him this way. Vane scrambled up the side of the nearest building, staying in the shadows as best he could like we had warned him to do. I wondered what the people inside thought about those claw noises.

All Vane had to do was get to the temple and come back with knowledge about what the Priestess used to reclaim her power. Once the fae knew, they could create a plan to go against it.

The rest of the fae joined in the battle while Tessa and his companions played around on the pyramid, frightening everyone there. Kala did the work of keeping all the cats safe, which wasn't so hard since the Eagle Warriors held spears, and they were not throwing them.

I didn't have any job except to watch and worry. Right then, I could have wished to be one of those cats; they at least got to take out frustrations by leaping and growling.

A warrior had fallen when he moved in the way of a magical attack. The others retreated to the safety of their leaders. The brightness of the magic blinded them, while the howls and screams drowned out the sound of flapping wings as Vane leapt into the sky and flew across to the temple at the top of the pyramid. He had to gain some height, and I watched, holding my breath. Vane circled in from behind, though. I saw him land on the roof; then he took his fae form and slid down, disappearing into the doorway.

I breathed a sigh of relief --

Lightning flashed within the building, and an eerie howl filled the air. Everything stopped on all sides. The cats laid their ears back and began to retreat. I stepped out of the shadows, shocked and afraid.

Vane appeared at the doorway to the temple. I thought he yelled something, but the unearthly sounds from within continued. The noises didn't come from him.

Vane transformed into the dragon and leapt straight at the Priestess. She screamed in fear.

I think everyone started screaming. Tessa changed back to fae and tossed magic at the woman, trying to draw her attention away from Vane. The jaguars, having lost their cat leader, scatted, while the Eagle Warriors turned on Tessa.

Kala raced up the ramp to reach him. A wave of her hand sent some of the warriors tumbling, but two others moved close to Tessa. The Priestess had cowered, but now she rose, shouted words, and lifted her hand. The magic hit Vane full in the chest, and he tumbled off the side of the pyramid, falling downward.

Tessa took a spear into his side.

York grabbed me. I didn't realize I had dashed straight for the danger until then. I don't know what he yelled. Brandis rushed to Vane and stood guard over him. The boy had changed back to fae form, but he laid without moving. Kala had hold of Tessa, fighting her way back off the pyramid as the warriors pressed in on one side and the priests on the other.

"Get them down!" I shouted to York.

I rarely give imperative orders, and York leapt to obey. While he moved up the ramp, I raced over and knelt by Vane. His chest moved with quick breaths, but I feared he had suffered from severe injuries.

I didn't expect Rose to lead a group to our defense. They made considerable noise, though they soon moved out of view. The sound had distracted the enemy long enough for Kala and York to get Tessa down beside Vane. Ember arrived, and along with Kala, York, and Brandis, she formed a square around the two Totems and me. Rose and her people retreated, keeping well out of the area near the pyramid.

We could not hold out for long. I saw the priests and Priestess coming down the nearest ramp and looking like gods descending from the power of the heavens to the dirt world of the humans. The woman gloated as she neared, knowing she had defeated us.

"Get -- Get Summerfield away," Tessa whispered. He held a hand to his side where blood flowed too fast.

"No," I said. "Can we get anyone else here? Is anyone left at The Fortress?"

Brandis shook his head. "Everyone who has taken an oath to you is here."

My heart pounded harder.

"Not *everyone*," I replied. I stood and decided on madness after all. Maybe my sisters were right. "Prince Arinith! I need you!"

"Oh hell," Tessa whispered.

I had just enough time to think maybe I could have come up with another answer before the temperature dropped about sixty degrees; a swift and frigid wind swept through the place, almost flattening us. Lightning arched across the sky. The Priestess grabbed hold of a priest when she almost fell.

Arinith arrived through a glowing portal just to the right of where we stood guard over our two fallen totems. He glanced around with a shake of his head.

"What the hell have you done this time, Summerfield?" he demanded.

"Need help!" I shouted. I had leaned down and grabbed Tessa as he fell back, almost unconscious.

"You know I don't dare do anything in this realm," Arinith replied, looking around with as much worry as the rest of us. "Nothing overt."

"Take Vane and Tessa with you --"

He looked up at the Priestess, who was not used to people arriving out of nowhere. She'd backed up in shock. Arinith at least bought some time as he stared past the woman with a frown.

"What do they have up there?" he said with a tilt of his head.

"We don't know," Brandis replied. They'd dropped the square -- no use wasting the power when they were not under attack. "Vane went to see. Then he attacked the Priestess, and she injured him, Prince Arinith. We would like to not lose him again so soon. Or Tessa."

Tessa seemed to grow colder in my hands. I had tried to stop the flow of blood while York worked on Vane. Kala knelt and did what she could for Tessa, but she didn't have York's extraordinary power.

Arinith's arrival had at least put the battle on hold. I still had hope that the Prince of the Fae, who held magic different than that used by the rest of my people, might find an answer. He didn't dare take any serious magical action in my realm because whatever he did would affect the world in dangerous ways. I had called him out of nothing more than desperation.

And he did two things. First, he reopened that portal to his own place and left it sitting there. Magic flooded through, and my fae grabbed at it, Kala working faster on Tessa until he breathed easier. I hoped that the magic had helped him, too. I couldn't tell.

Then Arinith did something odd. He turned to the High Priestess and pointed one of his long, thin fingers in her direction.

"You have made me very, very unhappy," he said.

Fae moods can affect weather in the human realm. My people had learned to dampen that side effect while in Omaha. In general, if you get a group of displeased fae together, then you'll get storms. Get one unhappy fae *prince* in place and...

A massive storm broke out over the top of us with a torrential downpour that a heartbeat later changed to ice and then to a blizzard of such strength that it almost took my breath away with the cold.

"Oh yes," Tessa mumbled. "This is so much better."

CHAPTER 18

While the others scrambled around in a panic, I grinned with delight. I held my hand out to the snowflakes.

"You are crazy if you like this, Summerfield," Kala accused. She looked increasingly frantic.

"There is something you haven't considered. We've been living in Omaha. We know about snow and ice."

"These people have never seen either," Tessa said. He struggled to his feet, but I saw a look of pleasure on his face.

I nodded and looked up at the pyramid. Sounds of dismay came from those above us as our enemies retreated as fast as they could, slipping on the ice, no doubt colder than they had ever been in their lives.

I did not feel sorry for them.

Arinith came out of the storm and helped carry Vane. I helped Tessa, and we retreated to the shop where we had first taken cover. Had that been just the day before?

Brandis cleared away enough debris so we could go inside. I looked back to see the Priestess head into the temple. A moment later, a small flash, like lightning within the walls, brightened the area. I suspected she wasn't having a good day.

Rose and the others had been nearby, and they scurried inside out of the weather, all of them cold. I wasn't sure of our safety, but I hoped Arinith would protect himself -- and those of us near him.

"If we left now, we could take the former slaves," I said as I looked out as the storm grew stronger. "We and leave this place. We'd protect them in the outer world. Would that be enough, at least for now, to keep power?"

"I think so," Brandis replied. His eyes narrowed as he glanced at Vane, who seemed better but still not conscious. That bothered me a great deal. "That would be enough to save the clan."

"But you don't think we should," I replied.

"I believe there is something more going on here that we need to consider."

"What is up there?" Arinith asked again as he stared out the doorway toward the temple.

"Whatever is there, it's hazardous," Tessa said. He settled against the wall with a hand to the wound but looking better. "We thought it was a well of power --"

"Something different." Arinith sat down beside us. I had expected him to leave, but I saw curiosity in his face this time. "There's a wrongness to it."

"They're powerful, Prince Arinith," Kala said. "We've tossed everything we have at them, and we haven't gotten through. Summerfield, I believe you may be right. We need to remove those whom we can get to safety and leave the enemy here."

"And what makes you think they'll stay?" Tessa asked. "Why wouldn't they follow?"

"They've never left this area before," I reminded him, but then I had a strange, worrisome foreboding. "But before this, they had no contact with any power from the outside. They were afraid to leave."

"Right." Tessa accepted a piece of fruit from Ember with a nod of thanks. "Now they know there are people with powers like their own out there, but not as strong. The Priestess is hungry for power and wants ours. What's going to stop her from following? We don't have the magic to stop her."

"Damn," I said. The others, including Arinith, nodded. "We have no way to trap them here?"

"Not that I have found," Brandis admitted. " I suspect that if we take her slaves, the Priestess is going to be mad enough to come after us, anyway."

Arinith still stared toward the pyramid, though the storm did not lessen, which made me suspect he wasn't as calm as he appeared.

"How is Vane?" I asked, looking over at him.

Vane had curled up asleep, as far as I could tell. He stayed in his fae form, which helped since we didn't have a chance of holding down a dragon.

"I think he'll be fine," York replied. "The injuries aren't serious -- but something upset him."

"Whatever he saw in the temple --"

I stopped. Everyone stared at me, expecting an answer. I had one, but I didn't want to believe it was true.

"Tessa, do you remember the mural in the tambo?" I asked.

"The journey one? I didn't understand the cultural implications, except that they were followers of Quetzalcoatl."

"Neither the Inca nor the Aztecs showed indications of

more than shamanistic magic back on the mainland. This group had power from the start once they got here. Where did they get it? We've seen no indication of power here except inside the temple that they built." The others nodded and waited. I took a moment to consider my idea, and then I plunged ahead. "I don't think they brought just their religion with them: I think they brought their god."

"Brought --" Brandis began.

"Oh hell." Tessa looked at me, at Vane, and back again. "Quetzalcoatl, the feathered serpent. A dragon of sorts. They have him trapped up there."

"That's my guess," I said. "The death of so many of his followers would have left him weaker at the time of his capture. What would it take to keep a god captive for centuries?"

"Just making certain he never got strong enough to fight back," Arinith answered. "But over time, he would weaken."

"I suspect that is why the Priestess wants ours," Tessa added.

"We must get him free." Brandis stood and paced to the doorway. "If we can do that, we won't have any trouble with the rest of these people."

We all nodded. No one voiced a plan.

"We must attack the temple," I admitted, saying what the others had avoided. I smiled when I saw Vane sit up. "Are you all right?"

"Dragon," he replied, with a wave of his hand as his eyes went wide. "Dragon with a spear in his side --"

"Damn them." Brandis stood straighter. "We'll fix this, Vane."

Brandis was the Warlord of the Dragon Clan, no matter what else he might be to me. The idea of a trapped dragon up there meant he must fix the situation.

I had better come up with a plan fast, or they would act even without a plan. Vane would not sit still for long, and he wasn't under my command. "The snow and ice unsettled them. We need to go straight up there and get Quetzalcoatl free before they recover."

They looked at me. Tessa started to speak. He paused and shook his head. Brandis was the next, but he stopped as well. Kala nodded.

"They're going to be off-balance," Brandis said with a wave of his arm toward the storm. "Literally off balance."

"She was afraid of me," Vane added. His voice trembled. "She thought he had escaped."

"Oh, that's a good point," Tessa said. "Do you think you could distract them again, but without getting hit this time?"

Vane smiled. I had not intended for him to go with us, but Tessa must have realized two things -- we couldn't make him stay behind, and he needed to know he could do something helpful.

Arinith didn't look as happy about it, and the weather showed his disapproval.

Better still.

I crossed to Prince Arinith before we left, though, and gave him a proper enough bow. He looked at me, more than a little curious about what I wanted this time.

"This is a dangerous ploy, but I see no other way of getting clear of here without things turning worse. The others, though," I said with a nod towards the ones who sat with my sisters. No, I did not introduce the Unholy Five. Or Paul, who stared in shock still. "Some of them have been slaves here for all their lives. I hope you will do what you can to help them."

He gave a gracious nod in return. "Don't take Vane," he whispered.

"He has to go. For himself," I replied with a glance at the boy. "He's not -- yet -- the Vane you knew. If we hold him back, will he ever be?"

"You never knew him." Arinith's eyes narrowed in anger. Lightning flashed through the air, and snow fell harder.

A whisper of worry passed among the fae as they looked at us with some consternation.

"You're wrong," I replied, which were not words Prince Arinith heard often. His eyes narrowed, but I rushed on. "I held the Dragon Clan Key. I knew Vane through it -- not as well as the rest of you knew him, but I still experienced the emotions of what Karolan had felt for him. That Vane would not have sat back and watched while others fought for something right."

"You are an annoying little human," he said with a shake of his head.

"Keep that in mind. We need the storm."

Arinith laughed. The others looked shocked.

We wasted no more time, except that York imbued us each with a little warmth. We headed straight out into the fierce wind and blowing snow. The ice proved treacherous, but my people knew how to handle it.

The Priestess stood with her most powerful priests outside the temple entrance. They would not let us into the building, and they knew we didn't have the magic to overcome them. They also had the source of their power at their backs. We had desperation on our side.

And Vane.

Vane once again came up over the top of the building, this time with a roar so loud people throughout the city heard him. The storm had left the pyramid glazed in ice and snow, a treacherous surface even for those of us who lived through Omaha's winter weather. Our adversaries trembled as much in terror as cold. We had brought our own god-like dragon into the battle -- one who was free and who had reacted in anger to what he had found in their temple. When Vane rushed down on them with his fierce call, it produced the reaction I had hoped. The people scattered across the ice with shouts of dismay. Two slid down several levels. Vane made an impressive twist in midair as he swept back at the Priestess who had lifted her hands.

She hadn't seen the rest of us coming up the ramp.

Kala and Brandis tackled her while Tessa and I rushed into the temple.

One rarely comes into the lair of a trapped god. I once woke a sleeping god -- Dagon -- but that was not the same. This place had an aura that made my skin crawl. Power surged through the building in layers of multi-colored rivulets of light. I felt as though we stood at the edge of a storm about to break open.

I heard the rasp of scales against scales, a subtle shift of movement. Two dark golden eyes stared out from the darkness. I wanted to pause and assess the situation, but we had little time. Vane could run into more trouble.

"There," Tessa said, pointing down the long edge of the glittering body. "That's how the bastards did it."

I saw nothing until I took a step farther into the shadows. Something glowed with a shaft of throbbing red light.

We could hear the growing frenzy of the storm and battle outside. I heard Vane sweep over again with another yell of defiance. No time. I took a step closer as my sight adjusted to the darkness.

"Careful, Summerfield." Tessa moved forward as well.

The tremendous hulking shape let out a hiss of anger as a flash of lightning filled the immense room. I saw what we faced for the first time, although my mind could not entirely take it all in. I saw a long snake-like form, scales glittering with silver and turquoise blue, while around the neck stood a ruffle of vibrant feathers in an array of reds, greens, and blues. The eyes, though bright as gold, did not stare at us.

I spotted the spear shoved into the serpent's side, resting against a sizeable golden basin into which the blood dripped in a slow, torturous release of power. As I watched in dismay, one glowing drop fell into the bowl. The sight appalled me, and I took another step closer.

"Careful," Tessa repeated as he moved toward me.

That won a brighter flash of lightning, this time far too close to Tessa. I realized he did not notice me at all.

"I'm not magical," I said, keeping my voice soft and steady. Did the dragon listen? Or had the mind slipped away long ago, leaving the poor creature deaf and blind? "I don't think he can sense me."

Tessa stared for a long moment before he gave a slight signal, almost as though he didn't want to. I took a step closer.

It didn't so much as twitch. However, when Tessa moved, he growled while lightning played along the edge of the walls.

I rushed most of the way across the room. They had driven the spear between the scales. It would have been agony to move. As I drew near, I could see the dull glow of runes carved into the stones and repainted with the dragon's own blood. I didn't think he could get out.

"Summerfield," Tessa said, his voice relatively calm. "I don't know what he's going to do --"

"Can you see the runes? Have they trapped him?"

"Runes?" Tessa knelt, peering into the darkness. "You're right. Good. Whatever you do, don't touch them. It could break the bond."

"That's what I thought."

I had gotten close enough now to reach for the spear if I dared. I decided, after all these centuries, that I should not move too quickly.

Kala rushed into the room. "Hey! We have a prob --"

She stopped, looked from Tessa to me standing by the dragon's side, and backed up.

"Never mind. We'll handle it."

"Good idea," Tessa agreed.

She turned and fled.

"I am going to move close enough to draw his attention," Tessa warned. We couldn't know if Quetzalcoatl understood us or not. I suspected he'd slipped beyond hearing the words of the humans who tormented him. "Can you pull it out?"

"It doesn't appear to be too deep. The bowl is a problem, but I don't think I dare move it."

"If this doesn't work, get the hell away," Tessa ordered.

He didn't often order me, but I knew enough to listen. "Ready?"

"Yes," I agreed.

I stepped closer, willing my hands to be steady as I reached for the spear. Tessa leapt forward, turning from human to cat in a heartbeat. I had expected him to do so, even if he hadn't said.

The change took the dragon by surprise, and it blinked as the head lifted. Not entirely gone, then -- just not paying attention. I rushed forward, grabbed the spear with both hands, and yanked.

There were two things we had not considered.

The first was that even a plain spear shoved into the side of a dragon god for several centuries would acquire some unusual characteristics. As soon as I put both hands on the spear, I felt a force try to take control. The fire of power surged straight through me as I jerked backward, and the spear came out.

So did a spattering of dragon blood, which proved to be the second problem. I had a sentient spear in my hands, and I also found myself linked with an enraged and insane god.

Quetzalcoatl screamed in pain. I screamed as well, but that came from rage. Tessa turned to me and then backpedaled in haste as I brought the spear up, ready to attack. He remained in cat form as he darted to the door and out into the storm.

The spear demanded we follow and strike. So did the dragon. Even though they both wanted the same thing, they fought for control of my body and created a backlash that froze me in place for a couple heartbeats. Then, at the battle's height, I shoved the weapon downward where the spear stuck three inches into the temple floor's hard stone. I let go of it.

That still left me with an overpowering link to the ancient God. I no longer had the weapon to help counter it. For a moment, we were both one.

I understood power. I saw a memory of creation and ... everything.

This was not something a human should experience. Part of my mind tried to pull back. If I didn't get clear of Quetzalcoatl, he would overcome me.

How did the Priestess and her people survive it?

One drop at a time.

The thought came unbidden. Quetzalcoatl's thoughts. I wondered how this had ever happened -- and in a heartbeat, I understood even that answer. The Spanish weapons had overcome him, just as they'd defeated his believers. Pizarro himself had helped smuggle the captive God onto a ship, though he thought it only a monstrous snake. Quetzalcoatl had shared his power on the journey, protecting his followers. Then the galleon had gotten caught in a storm, drove them to this island. With the help of the giant octopus, he and his people had escaped the enemy.

Quetzalcoatl brought them to the island, and then the priesthood trapped him. They didn't want to give up the power, and he had weakened himself so much that he could not fight back.

Trapped here for centuries.

I took a breath. Had I been breathing before this? I felt the burning spots of blood on my hands and realized I needed to get it off and break this link.

A storm still raged beyond the opening. I headed for the entrance.

Tessa, in fae form, moved to stand between me and the outside.

"Need -- wash off, Tessa," I said, gasping out the words. Did they echo through the building? I rubbed at spots of blood on my arms. "Need -- help --"

Tessa stepped back as I came out into the cold, and he saw that I no longer carried the spear. Tessa nodded with relief before his hands moved. Magic swept upward as he doused me in ice-cold water.

This was not what I'd had in mind, but it did the trick. I let out a cry of dismay and went straight down to my knees, trying to curl up. Tessa caught hold of me. Warmth replaced the chill of a moment before. The link to the dragon had disappeared.

My people still fought the battle out in the storm. I saw the Priestess make a desperate attempt to head back inside --

"No!" I shouted. A wave of my hand stopped her, even without any magic. "No, you will never stand before Quetzalcoatl again. You betrayed the trust of your God. You are unworthy --"

She heard something more than the words I said. She screamed, turned, and fled.

"Summerfield?" Tessa's hand tightened on my arm. "Are you okay?"

"It passes," I replied, while visions that were not my own played through my brain. Again. This felt more intense than my contact with the Dragon Clan Key, but it worked much the same.

"Rest," Arinith ordered. He sat down on the stone beside me. The storm died to a few last snowflakes in the sudden warmth and glare of sunlight. "Do you know what happened?"

"Quetzalcoatl," I said. I glanced over my shoulder toward the doorway. Something grumbled inside, and the sound sent a shiver through me.

"Summerfield?" Tessa asked, kneeling in front of me.

"Lord Summerfield is suffering from shock," Arinith said. The prince did something which he had never done before. He put a hand on my arm. "Be calm."

"Arinith," Tessa whispered, worried.

Before Prince Arinith's touch, I hadn't realized how *not calm* I felt. I had alien thoughts dancing through my mind, and closing my eyes did not help. In a flash of light and color, I relieved things that were not from my past and experienced them with far too much power. I didn't remember getting to my feet, but Tessa grabbed hold of me before I tumbled down the pyramid. Not something I wanted to experience.

"What do we do?" Tessa asked. He had not released me. I frowned, thinking I should order him --

No. That wasn't right.

"He has to come back on his own," Arinith explained. "He has to want to let go of his link to Quetzalcoatl and return to himself. I'm not sure that's going to happen. He's already had a major change. He might not know how to find himself."

Tessa looked into my face. "I'm sorry."

Something occurred to me. I was *not* sorry. Would I have wanted a sedate life? Or had my unusual life led me to this? Oddness didn't bother me.

I smiled. I saw Tessa's face change, and his relief washed over me. It was, I realized, nothing that Quetzalcoatl would ever have seen. He had followers, but I had friends.

"I need to sit down." I settled on the stone by Arinith once more. The warm sun beat down on my face. "What happened to the others? Where are the Priestess and the priests?"

"They are, very wisely, running," Arinith replied with a flick of his hand toward the jungle. "As soon as you withdrew the spear, they feared you would turn Quetzalcoatl loose. They knew there would be no mercy."

"Our people are chasing them off," Tessa added with a glance at the growth not far behind us. "I suspect the best we can do is make sure they can't return before their powers die out."

"That's going to be a long time," I warned and brushed my still-damp hair back from my face. "I learned that The Priestess and her companions have been tasting the power of the God since the start of the journey. They're all but immortal now."

"Damn. Should have thought of that," Tessa admitted. "Well, we'll keep them out."

"There's another problem," I added. "One besides having a more than insane dragon god on our hands. The spear has powers too. And it's just as mad -- crazy -- as he is."

"Ah." Arinith stared into the building at our backs. I had to work not to look as well, afraid of what might come after us. He shook his head. "Quetzalcoatl will remain weak for some time. I can't say how long, but it should help to get him calm before he breaks free."

That was another worrying thought. Quetzalcoatl hated humanity. How were we going to keep him from destroying every sign of humans that he could find?

This was a mess, and my people could solve it with a wave of a hand. I couldn't think of what to do, either --

Part of the answer arrived, soaring down to the pyramid. I smiled at the sight, glad to see Vane doing well. We'd come too close to losing both him and Tessa. And me, I supposed.

I saw something else -- how the people came out and pointed and then went to their knees believing Vane was, if not their God, at least one of his type. We would have to discuss the situation with Vane before he got ideas.

I looked at Arinith, who had watched where I did, and nodded. "I need to speak with Brandis. Are you better, Lord Summerfield?"

"Better. Yes."

He stood and headed down the ramp. Tessa took his place.

"I should have realized --" Tessa started.

"Because, of course, you deal with wounded gods so often," I replied.

"Well, not that," he admitted with a quick grin. "But I should have -- we both should have -- realized something would go wrong."

"Maybe so," I agreed. My hands trembled, so I put them in my lap where no one would notice. "But we had few choices, Tessa. No one else in our clan could have gotten that close. No, it's true. I know that for certain now. However, I also believe that another human, like one of my sisters or a local, would have been disastrous. I have dealt with another angry god, Tessa."

"True. We could have done something else --"

"There are many things we might have done in some other way," I said. "If we'd had time. We didn't. Now we have other problems."

He glanced my way, his eyes narrowed and his fingers twitching.

"Not me. I'll be fine. The real problem here, my friend, is not only how to deal with Quetzalcoatl as he gets stronger but also deciding how to handle all the people here in this city. We've known all along that we couldn't turn them out or open the island up to the outside."

"Keep it shielded," Tessa said. "That won't be so hard. The spell has been in place for hundreds of years, so now it's a matter of reinforcing it."

"Good," I said. Talking about things with Tessa helped ground me back into my world, strange as it might be. "We are also going to need to help restructure the society if they stay here. Should we instead bring the locals out into the world of modern technology?"

Tessa looked around. "Would that be fair?"

"I don't know," I admitted. "But we don't have to think about it right now."

"There might be something else we can do. I'll ask Prince Arinith if he thinks the fae could draw this island into their lands in a bubble that takes it out of this reality. The people who have only known this place would never have to leave it, and we wouldn't have to worry about future castaways."

"The fae can do that?"

"It is difficult, but there is a reason none of your

historians and archeologists have ever found Camelot."

I had never considered such a concept. Maybe I could visit, but that would be later. We had to fix this problem first.

"There are a few who came late and who know the outside," I said.

"We'll see what they decide. If those people want to go back, we can overlay their memories of this place with something else. Dangerous, but it should work. We can give them a different story to believe so that the tales of magic don't spread."

"Come on. It's time we get to work." I stood, and Tessa did as well. There was still some good we could do here.

CHAPTER 19

I would have thought we'd had enough adventure, and it was time to go home. Not quite yet.

Fae had spotted the Priestess and her powerful priests in the jungle nearby, but they'd not attacked. They wanted to get back into the temple and Quetzalcoatl. It would not happen. Even if they had found some secret passage inside, Quetzalcoatl was never alone. Dragon Clan members, including Vane, spent time with him. He seemed to understand that they were helping.

I, on the other hand, kept the damned Spear. It knew no manners and had a cat's attitude toward training. The ancient wood and copper tip also held enough magic that there would be no safe way to destroy it. I would have handed the weapon to one of my Fae, but right now, we needed everyone with real magic to work on the problems on the island.

We didn't dare leave it behind. Arinith would have taken it with him, but the thing refused to let Arinith even touch it. The Spear would go with no one but me. I at least convinced it to shape into a walking staff, though I could feel how it wanted to be a spear and taste the blood of others.

Great. I had a vampire spear.

The Fae had located my sister's lost luggage in that little overhang where we'd sheltered, and they changed clothes to nice pantsuits. I hadn't realized how much the show meant to them. Tessa and I just looked like wild men. It suited my mood.

Once we controlled the magic on the island, Kala left to talk to the Fae Queen and the other clan leaders in the fae lands to explain the situation. She had said the discussions would be tedious, but she knew they'd do the right thing when the decision came. Kala just had to suffer through all the bureaucracy first. I didn't envy her that duty while we helped the locals.

Then Brandis and Ember made a trip to the Fortress to check on things. They brought back more news.

"You six Summerfields can't show up in Omaha and pretend you had a fine vacation, even if you could explain the missing plane," Brandis explained as he sat down beside me, with the Spear between us. Brave man. "News of the disappearance leaked out yesterday, though the family had kept it quiet for as long as possible. Later, they confirmed that you and Tessa went with your sisters. You can imagine the reaction at the Fortress. We need to wind this up. Any word from Kala?"

"None," I said. The locals watched us with worry where we sat on the lower level of the pyramid. They knew we had defeated the Priestess and her people, so we were the new ones in charge. While I wanted to tell them they were free, I also realized how much their cooperation helped.

We worked hard over the next two days, preparing to leave, even if we weren't confident how we'd manage it. I did not go back to the temple, though it didn't matter. I felt Quetzalcoatl with me everywhere I went.

"They'll need guidance, those who had been slaves for so long. I can give it to them," Paul said to me late one afternoon. He had avoided me before this, but he had decided in a way I hadn't expected. "I have never found a place where I could do so much good. If I stay, will this be a problem?"

"No problem," I said and tried not to show my relief at his choice. "I think you'll do well. The Fae will be around, but they don't always understand humans. The locals are too used to taking orders from people with power, and we don't want that here."

"Thank you, Summerfield."

We shook hands.

Tessa wanted to make a link between the two places and pop us back to Omaha. We would need that portal since my Dragon Clan people were going to spend considerable time here, seeing what they could do to keep Quetzalcoatl calm and help him regain his sanity along with his strength. I didn't expect the work to be easy.

That afternoon, Tessa and I hiked back out of the city to look around. I stood on the stairs looking at this magnificent find -- that I could never share with others. I had accepted that part. However, I might at least use a few pieces to hypothesize how some Ancient American cultures had worked. I also still wanted to learn to read the knots in khipus.

I knew we had done something useful here. Despite the battle, storms, and earthquakes, I could see minor damage to the city. The Fae had helped with repairs, but locals did most of the work of rebuilding. They had started with the tomb of the Sapa Inca, and it looked magnificent again.

I turned and walked into the jungle. Before long, all signs

of the city had disappeared, and we walked on the stone-lined road. Tessa and I often took a walk to get away from everything for a few hours. This was my way of accepting that I would leave the island soon and return to the larger world as others took over the work here.

"Well, you have to admit it was an unusual vacation. Where do you think we should go next year?" I asked.

"If you ever say something like that again, I'm going to turn cat and bite you."

I didn't doubt it.

"Ember says the octozilla must have gotten some of Quetzalcoatl's blood when the original ship sank," I said. "It doesn't have powers, but it appears to have lived a long time and grown large. It shows no sign of leaving the bay. We will have to warn everyone to stay clear."

The staff trembled in my hand, wanting to take on the octopus, a worthy enemy --

"Stop that," I said as I pounded it against the ground. The surrounding area shook. "No, stop that, too."

The staff gave a brief twitch and stilled again. At least the Spear didn't sting me this time.

Tessa and I discussed some of what work we needed to finish here. He understood what the Fae could do, and I provided what I thought the humans would accept.

"As much as the fae might want to pull down the temple and the pyramid, I don't think that will be a good idea," Tessa said. "Well, they can't do anything about it at first, anyway. Quetzalcoatl is going to remain housed there for a long time."

"It's a focus for the locals, so we can use that to direct them. After Quetzalcoatl leaves, maybe they'll let it go to ruin in its own time -- but I doubt that will happen. They'll want it in excellent condition as long as they hold to the religion."

"We will stop sacrifices, human or other."

"Absolutely."

I should have known things wouldn't be so easy.

A storm grew across the sky in a sudden swirl of billowing clouds. I sensed Dagon in the wind. Dark clouds spread over us, turning the pleasant day into a chilly twilight. The local animals made calls of surprise before they went silent.

We had turned back to the city when the Priestess and her followers found us. She lifted her hand. Power filled the air as Ember and York arrived at a run, but she swept a hand and sent York flying. I heard him hit the ground with a grunt and get back to his feet.

I looked to the enemy. She stalked forward, her hand lifted as tame lightning flashed in her fingers. I had never seen such rage as I did in her face.

"You won't keep me out," she said, and the wind rose with her voice. I suspected maybe she had a bit to do with the weather as well. "Not after all my work. You cannot stop me --"

I tapped the walking stick, and it became a spear -- a familiar spear. She stopped, her eyes gone wide.

"Fool!" she shouted. "You have freed him!"

She attacked.

Tessa took on his cat form. He went for the Priestess, but he would not survive if I didn't do something. Ember and York had leapt at the priests, driving them back with fae magic.

I understood everything in with a single glance. The

Priestess turned a swath of lightning toward Tessa, but I moved with a speed that was unnatural for humans. I pushed Tessa away -- perhaps with too much force since he went flying off into the trees. The lightning that should have hit him came at me. I lifted the Spear and waved the strike aside.

She backed up a step.

"You have stolen the power from the God that should have been mine!" The Priestess screamed, her rage doubling. The wind shredded leaves and taking down small trees and bushes. I felt none of Dagon's influence now.

I saw no use trying to talk any sort of sense to this woman. She had lied to herself for centuries until it became a block she couldn't see around.

I brought the Spear up, poised to throw. It glowed red with power, and I could feel it ordering me to let it feast. We were going to have a long, serious discussion about this behavior ... later.

The Priestess screamed in rage and unexpectedly fled. One of her priests fell to Ember's magic and did not get back up; his body turned to dust. The others fled in terror. York had moved to stand behind her, ready for trouble, but they both relaxed.

"He'd been human," Ember said with a wave at the spot where the breeze already tossed him away. "He should never have lived this long."

"I wish we'd caught her. Tessa?" I said, looking around.

Tessa limped over to me, shaking his head.

"Next time, just yell for me to get down," he suggested.

We went back to the city, snarling at the sudden downpour, but not surprised. I hoped the Fae would hunt her down, but we'd learned that Quetzalcoatl's magic permeated the island, and she blended into the world around her.

I suspected that I would deal with the Priestess for a long time. Great. I'd add her to the list of other over-the-top crazy people who were after me, along with Gryn, Roan, and Dagon. I might include Quetzalcoatl, though so far, he seemed to appreciate that we were helping him.

The storm had at least cooled everything off. I also think Tessa was using some magic to keep the damned bugs away. We still had to bottle that stuff.

That night we had dinner in the ball court, as usual, welcoming any of the locals who wanted to join us. More arrived for each meal. They realized that life would be better now. Some protested when the slaves joined the feasts, but that changed as we discussed the work they were going to learn to survive. I forced them all into a new world of equality. They might think they'd go back after I left, but the Fae would still be here.

My sisters had been busy throughout the city, helping where they could -- but I could see the way each of them turned to me sometimes with consternation in their stares. All but Aster had families suffering from fear and loss. We had to do something.

And I thought I had a plan.

"How far off from the shipping lines are we?" I asked, looking at Brandis.

He blinked, but I knew he'd done some study for the Fae, just to make sure nothing we did here would cause trouble.

"About fifty miles from the current," he said.

"Are there any small islands close to it? Uninhabited

places with a few trees?"

"A couple, but not near enough that you'd draw the attention of a passing ship."

"That's not my plan. I think we need to build a raft and get out into the current. We can use magic to make certain we remain safe and to attract notice. It will have taken us time to build the craft, so we'll have a reason to have been missing for so long."

"That might work," Rose agreed. "As long as we'll be safe."

"That is no problem," Brandis said. "Well, at least if we can keep Dagon from getting crazy again."

I thought about being on a raft in the middle of the Pacific Ocean and one of Dagon's storms and immediately reconsidered the idea.

"It's still a good plan," Brandis added. "We'll keep you safe, even in one of his storms, as long as we know where you are."

"True. We need to get home. You'll have to come with us, Tessa."

"You want me, a cat, on a raft in the middle of the ocean with you."

"*Want* is not the word I would use in this case, but since everyone knows you were on the plane, you either have to take this part of the journey, or else you have to disappear out of our lives."

"Good point. So, we get to spend the last of the vacation basking in the sun, maybe eating a little sushi. I can stand that, I guess."

If only it had gone that well...

CHAPTER 20

S o, there we were out on the ocean for the fifth day in a row. We were all tired of the sea, the sun, and pretty much each other. The raft had space for a couple people to stretch out for sleep. We took that spot in turns. My sisters gathered at one end while Tessa and I sat at the front so Tessa could use magic to navigate. We had oars of sorts, but the craft drifted along in the current without considerable work.

We'd drawn the interest of a half dozen sharks that morning, and they circled us, moving in closer. I'd picked up the Spear. I wanted to dissuade them with such determination that I almost turned the thing loose. Instead, I leaned precariously at the edge of the raft, preparing to attack any of them that came too close. Tessa had magic ready.

The Spear dipped down in the water --

Every shark flipped over and swam away so fast that they threw fish up into the air in their wake.

"Well," I said and sat back.

The Spear was pleased.

On the fifth morning, clouds began building on the horizon. They grew out over the ocean surface, a line of gray against the glare of the water. I hoped that the weather would move off toward the west. I couldn't say the storm came from

Dagon, but I didn't like the look of it.

Kala dropped in with the day's main meal. We didn't suffer for want of food or freshwater. Kala even stayed for a while, giving news about the trouble we'd left behind. I thought she might be a touch too gleeful about our predicament, though.

"The Queen's Court has agreed to a provisional control of the island," she said as she sat down, handing out little baskets of food for everyone. Kala's deliveries had become the best part of our day. "The Queen is in favor of it, so that should persuade the others who are leery about bringing so many humans into the fae lands. No offense, but you are chaotic."

"Are you trying to tell me that the fae are not chaotic as well?" I asked.

"Only when dealing with humans."

"Ha."

Kala laughed. "Don't worry," she said, though she gave a narrow-eyed look at the growing clouds. "We've tracked two ships in the area. One is a research vessel, which we're nudging your way. The crew should spot you about sunset."

"Thank you," Tessa said, sounding appallingly sincere. He hadn't liked the ocean.

"The problem is that we don't dare mess too much with this storm because it might be obvious. The *Bright Cloud* is a weather research vessel."

"Just my luck," I replied but gave a little laugh. "At least this part is almost over. Thanks for the food. See you tomorrow if we don't get picked up today."

"We'll get all of you home soon, Lord Summerfield," she said with a bit more seriousness. Then she bowed her head and disappeared again.

The news of rescuers nearby put us in a better mood. I tried not to think about problems -- neither those we'd left behind on the island nor the ones we'd find when we got back home. We had enough to worry about right now because that storm looked dangerous.

Then, as the sun settled almost against the water, we saw the outline of the ship against the billowing clouds. A moment later, I knew they'd spotted us because people waved. The ship's horn blasted twice, and the craft turned.

Then the storm hit.

We were within half a mile of rescue when nature let loose with rain, wind, and enough lightning to blind us.

"Hold on!" I shouted to the others as I grabbed the edge of the raft. "We can still make it!"

In an odd twist of fate, my sisters listened to me, but Tessa -- who appeared crazed from the days on the ocean -- did not. Maybe he intended to use magic to help. He surged to his feet and lifted his arms, shouting what might have been a spell, though they sounded like words of rage. The raft rose upward on a wind-blown wave, then dropped downward. Tessa went tumbling toward the ocean.

I grabbed hold of him.

We both landed in the water. I heard my sisters yelling, but in the next moment, I found myself in the heart of the storm and the crashing waves. The combination swallowed up the world.

I grabbed Tessa by the collar, but he did nothing except sometimes move his arms. I feared we would go under at any moment, but I could at least wish us to float, right?

"Tessa!" I shouted but got too much water in my mouth. I coughed while I tried to shake him. " Dion Tessa! We need to get to safety!"

He might have said something. He still didn't help.

"Tessa, we're both going to drown!"

That drew his attention. Tessa blinked and then moved in a way that showed more awareness. I hoped he didn't change to his cat form because I doubted it would do any better in the water. If he did, I had to be prepared to let go so that Tessa had a chance --

A bubble of magic formed around us, bringing absolute calm amid the raging storm. At first, I thought that came from Tessa, but I realized the feeling was not at all right.

Dagon appeared, standing above the water with a glare on his face and his hands on his hips. "I will not have the others blaming me for this mess. We will continue our battle another time, Lord Summerfield."

He guided us to the ship before he disappeared. The storm returned, but I'd caught hold of the raft as the crew lowered a rope ladder. A young man scurried down to help as my sisters yelled and waved out toward the ocean. They hadn't seen us yet.

"We're here!" I shouted as I pulled myself up on the edge of the raft. Then I feared they'd do something dangerous to help us. "Get up so we can!"

Violet took charge, ordering the other four up while dragging Tessa up out of the freezing water. The Spear all but leapt into my hand. I thought about leaving it behind, but it would just find some other hapless person. I, at least, could control it.

"Look like part of the raft," I ordered as I made Tessa start climbing up ahead of me. "Don't draw attention."

The Spear wanted off the ocean, too. It obeyed.

I came up the rope ladder last. I had shoved the Spear into my belt and climbed up with no trouble.

"Souvenir of the raft," I explained as I pulled it out to use as a staff.

They took us into a room that looked like the mess hall, but equipment lined the walls, most of it chirping away as it gathered information.

"Must have been a glitch," someone said as we came in. "No sign of a calm spot now."

That would have been Dagon getting us to safety. I owed him for that one.

My sisters told our tale because I felt frazzled. The Flowers knew the story about the crash, the island, the raft, and our five days at sea. They told the tale well.

The *Bright Cloud* took us to Lima. We funded their next seven years of research. I'd found it fascinating and considered a new interest for another round of classes -- but then I thought about taking any of my fae out on a ship in storms. I decided maybe I'd just watch from afar.

We spent one day at the local hospital, where we were all pronounced remarkably healthy given our ordeal. Tessa managed to avoid most of the tests, so his not-quite-human physic stayed out of notice.

They sent us on our way.

We flew straight to LA from Lima, and from there, we took a private jet, but not to Omaha. We landed in Lincoln, hoping we wouldn't run into the hordes of journalists who had latched onto the story.

I'd arranged for everyone to meet at the Fortress since it sat on the road to the airport. We let out a rumor that we were flying in, hoping the correspondents would race to Epply while we took cover in the building. That way, my sisters could have some privacy for their family reunions. It wouldn't take long for the reporters to find us.

In fact, a couple of them might have been psychic. Two reporters had reached the Fortress ahead of our limo, but I don't think it hurt for them to see happy families hugging. Aunts, uncles, and our grandparents arrived in a line of limos and fancy cars. My friends had put together such a feast that we moved out to the park, where the reporters joined the festivities. Lenz even showed up. So did Julia, along with almost everyone else I'd ever known in the city.

We had an excellent homecoming.

Four days later, things turned strange again.

"Just get to the courthouse, Sunflower," Rose said on the phone. "You and Tessa if he's around. There isn't much time. You need to be here."

"What --"

But she had already ended the call.

So, Tessa and I went to see what the lawyers were doing. My fae didn't allow me out alone yet, since we might have trouble from various old gods. Kala and Brandis both came along, but they stayed in the car after they dropped at the door. Lily stood waiting inside and ignored my questions as we rushed toward the stairs.

"Just come on. No time!" Lily began taking the steps even faster. "Judge Bridges has the case. She won't wait."

"Fine," I said. We went with Lily. At least all of us were in good shape after our *vacation*. We arrived in a courtroom to find Cousin Tommy's hearing in progress. His lawyer had just placed a paper into the Judge's hands when Lily ushered us in. Rose stood before the Judge and looked relieved. I thought someone would protest our intrusion. Bridges scowled, but she read the paper and then gave me a steely-eyed stare. I remembered that Tommy boy had named me as his drug dealer and felt a chill.

Was the Judge about to charge me? That seemed unlikely, but there were several police officers present. I didn't know the full implications of what Tommy had already said, having forgotten this problem.

Lily and Tessa took seats back from the proceedings. I just stopped in the aisle, not sure what I should do.

"Sunflower Breeze Summerfield," Judge Bridges said as she crooked a finger for me to come before the bench.

What the hell?

Tommy looked smug. So did two people sitting behind him -- Jacobs and Kenwood.

Rose stood by the other lawyer. She gave me no indication of what was going on.

"Mr. Summerfield --Sunflower Summerfield -- do you know why you are here?"

"No clue at all, Your Honor."

She nodded.

"I have a deposition here from Thomas Summerfield, which is also signed by two others who witnessed the event. As part of his plea to avoid jail time yet again, he agreed to give up his drug dealer's name. The paper says that six days ago, he bought illegal drugs from you and Dion Tessa, which were found in his car the next day."

She handed the paper to Rose. Rose let me read it with her.

We gave it back.

"I assume you have something to say?" Judge Bridges said.

"Other than he and his two companions are idiots?" Rose asked. I had never heard of her utter anything so inappropriate in a courtroom. Tommy's lawyer made sounds about insults while Jacobs and Kenwood smirked.

Well, right until they saw me smile.

"I heard that the news reports were late in adding that Dion Tessa and I were also with my sisters on that plane trip. From as often I've seen it played, I would have thought they'd seen the video of all of us being picked up by the *Bright Cloud* on the day he says I sold the drugs to him here in Omaha."

"Your sisters," Tommy said, his voice rising in sudden panic. "Just your sisters --"

"Even I have seen the video uploaded from the research vessel. I read the reports from Lima, not to mention the arrival in LA," Judge Bridges said. "Quite a story, detailing your crash, building a raft, and the days on the ocean. I suspect I will see a movie version in the future."

"Oh, dear God, no," Rose replied with genuine dread. Then she took a deeper breath. "Though this would make a nice postscript to the story. I believe, Your Honor, that we will clear Sunflower of most, if not all, the other dates presented by Thomas Summerfield.".

"The date is wrong," Tommy all but shouted, surging to

his feet as though his brain realized the depth of trouble he faced. "I must have gotten it mixed up. I was confused. The drugs he kept selling to me -- I --"

"I suggest you shut your client up, Mr. Herman. Oh, don't even think about leaving, Mr. Kenwood and Mr. Jacobs. We're going to be handing out all kinds of jail time here."

"We didn't do anything!" Jacobs complained with growing panic.

The Judge held up the piece of paper. "You said you witnessed the sale. Notarized and everything. Thank you, Rose Summerfield, for getting your brother here to refute the charges in person. It was so much more enjoyable."

"I appreciate you calling me in when you realized the kid was going to have to face this latest harassment. I'm glad to have it handled so well."

"If you'd care to stay --"

"No, thank you," Rose said. I nodded in agreement. "We will leave this in the court's hands."

Rose led us out. We kept quiet all the way out the front door of the monumental building. Then Rose gave a shout of pure delight, a sound like I'd never heard from her before.

"Oh, that was joyous," Rose said with a laugh. "I'm sorry for Aunt May and Uncle Chad, but damn -- they're better off with Tommy boy out of their hair for a while. Jacobs and Kenwood so wanted to be there when they brought you down that they wandered into this drama like little sheep to the slaughter. I now believe in Karma, Kid. I really do."

So, it was a win all the way around.

As soon as we got home, I threw myself down on the sofa with a sigh of relief. Most of the others were there and had tea ready. Brandis had set up a regular rotation of mostly Dragon Clan members to watch over our unusual island. However, Vane was back to the Fortress, which pleased me. Everything felt normal again ... at least, for our definition of normal. The Gremlins joined us, running around the room in a game of tag. They even grabbed some cookies that someone had 'forgotten' and left on the counter.

They whispered and then brought a cookie to me and one to Vane.

Well.

Vane sat on the sofa beside me. I suspected he'd made another of those leaps in growing up again. He didn't appear to have changed in appearance, but there was a sense of calm in his face that I hadn't seen before.

"There's considerable work to do back there," he said with a vague wave in the island's direction. "But I understand it will take time. I am learning patience."

"It's something difficult to deal with sometimes," I admitted. "I wish --"

Tessa launched himself from halfway across the room. Vane had already thrown himself over me. The others laughed, and the Gremlins joined in, piling on top of us. It's a wonder I didn't have broken bones by the time we untangled.

I pushed everyone off and stood. "I think we should go have pizza."

No one argued.

So, all returned to normal, except for two minor problems -- and no, it isn't the Spear. I've got it under control.

My sisters began taking lessons in the Fae Law Code and have set up an office at the Queen's Court at her invitation.

And Aster and Tessa are dating.

Some things are just too scary to think about.

THE END

PREVIEW: RAVENTOWER & MERRIWEATHER 1: SECRETS

CHAPTER ONE

With a careful nudge of the delicate pick, Mica slid a minuscule gear inside a casing no larger than a silver coin and maneuvered the cogs into place. They clicked together; he pulled the pick back and let go.

The larger gear swept counterclockwise, drawing the smaller one in a half circle ... and forward again, and back again, the balance perfect. Click-click, click-click: the sound of a clockwork heart come to life.

The ancient sea metal from which he had made the last gear glowed softly with a hint of blue that reminded him of distant stars. The light indicated a magical power which he still couldn't analyze despite years of study. The unusual metal would keep the little heart beating for as long as the gears remained in place. An immortal clockwork heart rested in his hand; soon it would have a body, and one day it might even have a soul.

With the delicate work done, Mica looked up from his desk and blinked as his mind connected once more with the world around him. A faint hint of a sea breeze rustled papers placed beneath a fluted shell to his right and reminded him of estate work he still had to do. He let his fingers brush over the papers, but he didn't draw them out or retrieve the ledger from the cabinet.

The room felt cooler than it had been when he started the clockwork project and a glance at the barometer on the wall showed a drop in pressure, forewarning of a storm to come. The partially open windows let in the early afternoon light along with the distant sounds of both the city and the sea as a temple bell rang on one side of the tower, and a seagull shouted on the other. The bell marked the third hour of the afternoon, and he'd have to light the gas lamps soon if he continued to work. Best to take advantage of the daylight while he could, even if the breeze hinted at a storm coming, and perhaps even ice and snow.

Mica glanced at the other gears laid out on his work table and mentally inventoried what remained and how to put the pieces together. This one next, and then another, and. . . .

He bent back to the work, noted the fourth-hour bell in passing, and continued on.

Sometime later he heard the flapping of mechanical wings near the window and then the click of metal claws on the stone windowsill. Mica refused to look up from his work although he grimaced at the intrusion. The unnatural bird shoved open the window which had only let in a faint hint of fresh air so that a sudden icy breeze blew in from the seaward side.

Click-click-click; the bird would not be ignored for long. With a barely concealed sigh, he gave a negligent nod and went back to work.

"A message," it said with a grating voice. Mica thought the clockwork bird might be in need of some oil. "From Prince

Gregorian to his brother Lord Raventower."

Mica snorted. His brother never left off their titles, carefully pointing out his elevation in status since he'd married the king's daughter.

"Continue." Best to get this out of the way, though he didn't look up or stop his own work.

"Prince Gregorian requests that you come immediately to the castle."

"I'm sure he does," Mica mumbled and bent closer to his work.

"He said to say please."

Surely the world had just stopped.

Mica lifted his head, pushed his chair away from the worktable, and instinctively pulled the wooden cover into place over the delicate array of gears and casings. His shoulders and neck protested the movement as he turned his head.

The brass raven standing on the windowsill was one of his more elaborate creations, though that was not what allowed the creature to take orders or to talk. People thought them wondrous that they flew, but they would have called the four ravens unnatural if they knew the rest of what they could do.

And they were unnatural, but that was not Mica's fault. Not exactly.

The ravens served him well, even if they did sometimes bring him messages he didn't want to hear. Mica glanced out the window towards the city, looking past the gray soot from thousands of chimneys until he could pick out the towers of the castle in the far distance. The impressive building sat atop a higher hill than his own tower and at the other side of

Kamere -- a long journey on a late, cold afternoon.

Though the king ruled the country of Sedina, Lord Raventower was the local noble for the city of Kamere and the adjacent lands. The Raventower lands had been without a lord for twenty years before Mica had taken up the role hardly two years before. His older brother would have been invested as Lord Raventower, but he had married the King's daughter and became a prince instead.

The bird moved again, his mechanical wings fluttering slightly and the claws tapping almost nervously on the stone.

"Fly back and tell Gregorian I'm on my way," Mica ordered, giving in to the inevitable.

The mechanical raven gave one quick bow of his metallic head, the red eyes glowing as it turned and flew away. The bird would reach Prince Gregorian far faster than Mica could make the trip, being earthbound and hindered by the maze of streets he would have to traverse between Raventower and the King's Castle.

No time to waste. Gregorian's far-too-polite request meant something dire had happened and most likely included a death. The King's? He hoped not. The Queen's? One of their children? He prayed to the Gods and Goddesses that it was not Gregorian's wife or one of their children.

With growing anxiety, Mica shoved the window all the way closed and then crossed to the pull cord that stood by the huge, unfinished clock built out from the north wall. The legend above the unmoving clock face mocked him: Will Tell Time was spelled out in carefully chiseled letters. His late father had designed and begun the clock and Mica still couldn't get the device to work. Mica still relied on the distant sound of bells from the Temple of Justice and counted the hours like a commoner.

He pulled the cloth-covered rope three times and heard the deep resounding bell catch with each swing. Three times only -- his stableman would know to have the carriage ready by the time he descended from the top floor of Raventower to the courtyard below.

He did not exactly run down the ancient, well-worn stairs that had been made slick by hundreds of years of use. The massive square tower was older than the city since the village of Kamere (then called Ravenroost), had grown up around the huge building.

Though the structure still proved steady enough, the interior was in sad need of repair, having been abandoned for twenty years. The late Lord Raventower -- whom Mica had never known, despite being his son -- hadn't cared much about the upkeep before his death, either. The man had made a few modern improvements, but with little regard for how well the additions melded into the rest of the building. The gaslight lines ran ugly pipes up the outer walls across the stairway landings, and along the inner halls so that they looked like some creature snaking his way through the building. Mica had to be careful not to grab or bump them since some were corroded and needed to be replaced.

The gas lighting was an improvement over candles and oil lamps, but the work of replacing the entire system would be difficult, especially if he wanted the workmen to do a better job.

Mica reached the ground floor, five floors down from his tower workroom. There he found Ada, the cook, waiting by the ancient and intricately carved double doors that opened out to the courtyard.

She held out a small, cloth-wrapped package. "Eat this on your way, your Lordship. You've had little else today."

Ada took good care of him despite his eccentricities. Mica smiled and took the package then grabbed his long wool cloak by the door.

As he opened the door, a blast of icy wind blew off the sea to his right. Mica should have thought about the weather change, but once the importance of his brother's message struck him, he hadn't thought of much else.

"Ada, have the shutters put on the windows in the workroom please," he said as he pulled the cloak over his shoulders.

She gave a curtsy and hurried off to order the work done. Ada was the one who truly ran Raventower. He only kept a couple servants, but even if there had been dozens, Ada would have taken control. He watched the tall, thin woman hurry off.

The handsome rosewood carriage sat in place across the courtyard, and the two massive clockwork horses of bright brass and copper were almost hitched. The elegantly sculptured lines of the clockwork steeds still thrilled him as much as they had the first time he had sketched them out on paper. Roe kept Kandris and Lestian polished and the gears well-oiled. Live horses rarely got as much care as the stableman gave to these two constructs.

"We're ready, your lordship," Roe said, giving the harness a last tug. He wore his massive cloak against the cold as well as thick gloves and a scarf, but the man's neatly trimmed black beard showed a hint of white frost from the cold, damp air.

Summerfield 4: Spring Break/253

"Where do we go, sir?"

"To the castle." Mica climbed up on the foot board of the oversized Brougham and paused. He tried very hard not to sound worried, but Gods, this might be serious. Gregorian would have sent an ordinary messenger for anything mundane, and he would not have asked to please come to the castle. "Make the best time you can, within reason."

"Yes Sir," Roe said, pushed the door closed after Mica, and climbed up to take the reins.

Mica looked back at the tower as they made the slow turn towards the gate. The tower stood square and ancient, the windows narrow and a huge stone raven with folded wings stood sentinel on each of the four sides. The stone had darkened through the ages and it held none of the beauty of the more modern buildings of the city, including the Kamere Castle.

Mica pulled the window shade down and took his usual place on one of the two facing benches. The comfortable black leather interior had been built to his specifications and hid a few secrets, like the horses that drew it. No one but he understood how his mechanisms worked.

He devoured the sweet cake Ada had given him before they were through the Raventower Gate and on the short, angled road that descended to the noisome level of the city.

Closed into the dull interior, with only a little light slipping in around the shade, Mica sat back and listened for other bells. There would be bells ringing in all ten of the major temples and most of the lesser ones if one of the royal family died. So far the city remained blessedly quiet, except for the usual throb of life when over a million people gathered too closely together.

As the road evened out -- if one didn't count the constant bumps of the cobblestone -- the buildings rose up and blocked out most of the light, even the little that came through the pulled shades. Mica edged open the shade on the window opposite the door and watched as they passed familiar buildings, the colorful doors and trim dulled in the growing darkness. The scent of burning wood nearly overcame the less pleasant odors. Sounds that had been a distant hum in the tower became voices yelling and fading again as they passed, the thrum of factories becoming a dull roar that almost overcame the thunder of steam engines. He heard other vehicles, including a steam trolley with the loud horn that could startle horses and humans alike. No one seemed used to the steam-powered vehicles, even more than ten years after they'd been introduced to the city.

His own vehicle drew notice, of course, but for entirely different reasons. The Raventower coat of arms adorned the doors, and the black and gold pennant fluttered over the driver's head, giving everyone fair warning to move out of the way. However, the clockwork horses, the only two in existence, drew the most attention. He had been offered several fortunes for the two or ones like them. People had no idea what it took to create such mechanical beasts.

Hovels and factories lined the road here, including the dark opening to the Shadow Walk, an infamous section of town where no one uninvited went. He watched as they passed, seeing shadows moving in shadows. The people who made their homes along that desolate path were not toyed with by anyone, even the city guard. They were not so much evil as simply desperate, and when someone had nothing to lose, even the authorities were slow to push them into doing something drastic.

Mica hated that such destitution existed at the foot of his tower. The factories, belching black smoke into the sky both day and night, did no better for the overworked employees than they did for the city air.

They passed Shadow Walk, passed factories, and passed people trudging their way home in the dimming light, hurrying before the coming storm that they read in the message delivered by the growing wind.

The road got a little better. Roe picked up speed. Between the poorer part of town and the better area stood Temple Square which was always kept in good repair. Roe cut through the edge of the vast plaza, the place thronging with priests wearing robes of various styles and colors to indicate the God or Goddess they served. Even here Mica sensed a touch of urgency, heads turned to stare at the clouds pushing in from the sea. The gathering at the Temple of the Wild showed that many residents, rich and poor, were praying to Kiminson tonight and hoping the coming storm would pass quickly.

Roe dared not rush through the lingering crowd, many of whom gathered to see the wonder of his metal horses. The massive bell in the tower of the Temple of Justice rang out the sixth hour. The sun had already started down, and the impending onslaught of the storm made the coming night seem dire.

Mica scowled at the growing dark and then dropped back on the seat. He drew a flint from his vest pocket and lit the little lamp that hung down from the ceiling though the device swung and danced as they moved. He also drew out a half dozen small gears from his jacket pocket and toyed with them to keep his mind busy. He would much rather have been back at his worktable.

The thought reminded him that he was not quite prepared to visit the castle. A high lord did not enter the august building with frayed sleeves, oil smudges on his fingers, and dust on his clothing. He kicked the bench in front of him, and the top popped open. Inside he kept an array of good dress shirts, some finely scented cleaning oil, and a hair brush. This was not the first time he'd been called to the castle on short notice, and he would not risk another mortifying lecture by his older brother who seemed to think Mica was still nine or ten.

He cleaned his hands, put on the best of the white shirts and had just pulled on an elegant black vest and straightened the lace on his sleeves when the window by the driver's bench opened and Roe leaned down to look in.

"Pardon, your Lordship, but I see Shipley and Bear at the next corner, and they look like they might ha' run a bit to meet us."

"Stop and let them in," Mica said, feeling a surge of dread. Surely the street boy didn't know what was happening at the castle!

The carriage slowed and stopped. Roe leapt down and opened the door so the boy could get right in with the least amount of time wasted. The area beyond the door appeared deserted for the moment, so the boy had timed the meeting well. While people knew Shipley sometimes bought and scavenged scrap metal for Lord Raventower, the two did not advertise that the exchanges often went beyond metal to information.

Shipley scrambled inside. Though in his early teens, Shipley was small for his age and looked like he might be ten or eleven. The boy had a good head on his shoulders beneath that mop of poorly cut brown hair.

"Your Lordship," he said with a quick nod as he pulled himself to the far side of the bench opposite him. Mica had done the same, making way for Bear.

Bear had sometimes been mistaken for the animal for which he had been named. The huge dog threw himself into the carriage which rocked with the sudden jolt. Standing on all four legs, Bear's head reached almost as high as Shipley's shoulders. The massive body, covered with long brown and gold fur, made the animal look formidable. He would have been taken from the boy long ago except that Bear had a lame back left leg. Besides, anyone who had tried to part them had been in for a surprise when the normally docile dog turned angry.

Bear dropped down on the floor and gave a contented sigh as the carriage began to move.

"You were looking for me, Shipley?"

"Heard you were about, me Lord," he said with another quick nod of his head. No matter how often they met, the boy always seemed worried he would do something improper. "Had a bit a' news. Two Atria ships made in at the floating dock this afternoon and a third just slipped in no more than a bell ago. Sailing ships, not steam, so they look like merchants, and I heard say they're tellin' others they took to land to avoid a storm brewin'. Thing is, they be ridin' awful low. They say they won't trade here and won't let inspectors aboard. The patrol are keeping an eye on them."

"If they're not trading, it's their right not to be inspected." Mica frowned and pulled the edge of his cloak out of the way before it became covered in fur. "Claiming they're running before a storm, though -- that I mistrust. Atria ships, coming from so far north, are made to sail in storms. So either there's a hellish storm out there or they're here for a different reason. The guard is alert, at least."

"Thought so, too," the boy said with a nod. Shipley pulled a small leather bag from his pocket and held it out. "Not much o' the fancy metal this time, but a few nice gears and such bought at the beggars' market yesterday."

"Good work," he said, glancing inside. The few small pieces of the ancient metal glittered a bit in the near dark. He fetched out a dozen copper coins and handed them over before he pushed the bag inside his vest. "And if there is a storm --"

"I'll get me mates down on the shore looking for sea metal scraps after it passes," he replied. "Best be off here afore we get to somewhere busy like. You're out late, though, ain't you?"

"My brother sent word for me to come to the castle," he said. It was only fair; they traded metal for coin and information for information. Shipley had already told him about the ships. "I have no idea what this is about, but it might be important."

"Ah. I'll listen about, then."

Mica tapped the wall by the driver's seat three times and the carriage came to a stop. Shipley opened the door and looked anxiously outside, gave one quick nod, and jumped out.

The dog made an awkward turn, the carriage tipping left and right before he followed the boy. Mica reached out and caught the door handle, but the two had already nearly disappeared into the shadows and growing fog.

Before he got the door closed, a woman stepped out of the shadows: dark clothing beneath a black cloak and a face as pale white as a winter moon. She looked his way, and he found himself staring into her equally dark eyes.

"You must work on time," she said, the words soft but clear.

Then she turned and walked away as well.

Roe, having seen the boy and dog leave the carriage, had already started moving. Mica held to the door and leaned out, trying to see where the woman went until he nearly tumbled into the mud and muck. He pulled himself back with a start and slammed the door shut and latched it.

He would ask Shipley about the woman next time they met. He didn't want to worry about anything else odd tonight. He purposely spent the rest of the time carefully tidying up and preparing for his visit to the castle. The King or Queen might be there.

He didn't want to do anything improper -- and he felt a bit of kinship with Shipley with that thought.

Now that they were well past the Temple Square, the road was better kept and less likely to twist and turn. They passed through the market streets, the buildings closed up and the street booths down for the night. Trollies screamed their whistle cries at every corner and a small steam bike darted past them and headed up the hillside with a roar of power, probably moving close to fifteen miles per hour.

Fewer people appeared on the streets in this area, and most of those he saw were day laborers heading back to the poorer parts of town. The richer segment of the city had already taken cover behind the high estate walls, safe from the wind and cold. Roe had no trouble along the wide King's Way Road and the clockwork horses even picked up speed despite that they were going uphill. A shame the steam bike had disappeared. They could have raced.

By the time the carriage climbed up the last steep hill and reached the first of the two castle gates, a robust northeast wind had begun to blow in off the sea and howled around the curtain wall of the huge set of structures. Rain splattered against the wood and Mica considered himself lucky to have gotten this far before the clouds let loose.

The guards at the gate barely looked inside the carriage and passed him on into the passage way that led to the second gate and the courtyard. The path wound through a plethora of storage buildings and smithies that seemed to have sprouted up like mushrooms in a boggy forest. The wind already tore at the makeshift thatch roof of one shed and soldiers handed up bags of grain to hold it down.

As soon as they reached the outer, processional stairs, Mica threw himself out of the carriage and forced the door closed. He held his cloak tight and looked up at Roe, huddled against the cold.

"Leave the carriage and come up to the entry and some cover. The weather isn't going to hurt the horses, you know, and they aren't going to take off without us."

"Yes, your Lordship," the driver agreed. Roe climbed down and pulled his own cloak close as they went up the ten rain-slick steps to the entrance.

Before Mica could pull the bell, Prince Gregorian himself pushed the door open and with his companion's help, fought it back closed again. Roe gave a bow to the Prince and Lord and settled on the bench by the door, content to be inside.

"Damned bad storm to blow up out of nowhere. Maybe the Atria were right to come to port after all," Gregorian mumbled as he started off, moving at a brisk, steady pace that was only a fraction off from a jog.

Prince Gregorian, who was also a General in the Sedina Army, tended to march wherever he went. He wore his uniform today, as usual, the straight black trousers, black boots, white shirt and black vest immaculate. This was the standard clothing for the Guard, at least in various degrees -- foot soldiers did not wear black silk vests with gold buttons. Over the vest, he wore the pristine white jacked that marked him as a General. He preferred that title to Prince since he had earned it in some hard fields of battle.

That General Gregorian almost ran through Kamere Castle worried Mica all the more, though they did not take the stairs upward, but rather headed into the older twisting halls of the ground level. This was not a place where they were likely to find the body of one of the royal family.

Oil scones dotted the ancient stone walls here, darkly staining the areas around them with centuries of smoke and seemed to make the passages even darker. No gaslight pipes had been brought into the palace where the royal family had a fear of explosions, either accidental or intentional. This level was a warren of halls and small rooms used by people who kept the castle working, from paperwork to clean linens.

Servants were used to seeing Gregorian in the area and moved out of his way then went back to their jobs with hardly more than a bow of their heads. Lord Raventower, rushing along in his wake, was no stranger either, having spent all but the last two years of his life in the castle. They didn't pay him much attention at all.

Gregorian stopped and gave a nod to a woman in a Guard uniform and wearing the red jacket of a lieutenant. The black corset beneath the jacket showed a line of decorated pins down the front; this one was no ordinary guard. She'd seen more than a few campaigns though she looked no older than Mica. Pockets embedded in the leather corset showed the handles of small throwing knives, a weapon most never became adept enough with to rely upon in battle. She wore a sword on her left hip and a flintlock at her left right, with a black powder case across her shoulder. This was a formidable soldier. The woman gave General Gregorian a quick hand-to-heart salute and stepped aside without even acknowledging Lord Raventower.

There, in the corner of the dark hall, Mica spotted the body he had been dreading from the moment the raven had uttered that please.

This was not what he had expected.

The face turned towards him was an older man with a bald head, the fringe of a gray beard, and a prominent nose. Mica didn't know him. He wore the gray robes of a Priest of Eligeius, the God of the Known. The priests of that temple were little more than glorified historians, archivists, and tutors.

They rarely rated a knife through the heart.

"What is going on?" Mica finally asked.

"That's what I hope you can tell me," Gregorian said his voice gruff and hinting at frustration. Gregorian never handled frustration well. He looked at the guard and pointed the way they had come. "Merriweather, go to the corner in the hall and make certain no one disturbs us."

"Yes, sir." Her glance towards Mica lingered but she asked nothing. Good soldiers did not question why their commanding officer pulled his eccentric younger brother in to look at a murder.

"I have a guard at the other end of the hall as well, and no one has been near the body since they called me in. I got you here as quickly as I could," Gregorian said, his voice softer now. "I don't like that this has happened at a time when we have strange Atria ships, even if they are a quarter mile out at the floating dock -- and rumors of a fleet not far away. I want to know what reason someone had to kill this priest."

Gregorian knew what he asked. This wasn't a quiet death. The murder of anyone in the palace was reason enough to want answers quickly, whether there were Atria in the harbor or not.

Mica had kept back from the body until now, but with a quick glance to make certain no one lingered nearby, he dropped his cloak by the wall and stepped forward to kneel by the dead priest. He kept his hand steady as he reached out and his fingers brushed over the forehead.

He had arrived almost too late already after the long journey from one side of the city to the other, and the links he sought were indistinct. He sensed the cold of death first, like ice invading his hand and arm. A moment later came the faint sparkle of life lights drifting up around his hand, the dimness showing that most of the essence of this man had already gone on to whatever reward the God of Knowledge promised his followers.

Mica put his other palm flat against the too-cool skin of the head and closed his eyes, concentrating on whatever little bit of memory he could catch. The moment of displacement came at last when it seemed his own life became nothing but a shadow, and another tried to take over, though at least this one was already fading. Mostly he found contentment. Anxious to get back to the temple before night set in. Worry about the storm.

Then a moment of surprise that verged on shock --

Darkness. Death had come quickly after the surprise. Mica tried moving his hand, hoping for a little more, and caught a whisper about a pleasant lunch.

"Careful, Mica," Gregorian warned, drawing his attention back to here. "Someone coming."

Footsteps rushed their way. Mica glanced down the hall and found the woman, Merriweather, coming at a near run.

"General Raventower, your sister --" But she stopped when she saw Mica, the faint glow of flickering lights still gathered around his fingers. "Oh."

She didn't need to say more in warning. Mica stood, pulling away from the body in haste and letting go of the tie. The lights began to fade, but he knew the display would not disappear quickly enough.

Priestess Honoria Raventower turned the corner into the hall and spotted her brothers. Her step quickened, and the immaculate white of her Robes of Justice accentuated the bright red of rage in her face. Mica stopped himself from taking a step backward as the last of the life lights faded from his hand. Gregorian, braver than his younger brother, stepped forward.

"Honoria --" Gregorian began.

"I saw." Her blazing hazel eyes turned to Mica and locked on him as the rage grew. The resemblance to Gregorian, her twin brother, was apparent at this range, though she had none of his control. Her eyes nearly bulged with fury as she moved past Gregorian and faced Mica. "What did you have to do with this death? Answer me!"

Mica had been so shocked by the words, which made no sense to him, that he'd paused, waiting for her to rephrase the question. He should have known better: she had meant exactly what she said.

The thought that she would accuse him --

"I had nothing to do with the death," he said, his voice calm and unnaturally quiet, a personal wall against her rage.

"Then what are you doing here!"

"I sent for him," Gregorian replied, his own voice almost matching hers in anger. "I needed answers --"

"So, you called him, let him use his foul, dark magic --"

"I have no magic," Mica interrupted, though not to convince her. Others were gathering, drawn by her arrival and the loud, angry words. This wasn't the first time he'd had this discussion with Honoria, for all the good it ever did him. She was all but shouting now, and he truly wanted this confrontation contained and ended quickly. "I have neither studied nor sought the path of magic of any sort. Whatever I can do is a Gift of the Gods, likely passed down through our mother --"

"You are lying, Micalus! Don't you dare lie to me."

Mica met her glare this time and didn't look away. "I thought you were a Priestess and Justice in the temple of Dina. I thought that meant you could tell the truth when you heard it."

Mica hadn't used this tactic before, and he wasn't certain if the words had been wise. Honoria took her position as a priestess and judge very seriously. He had come close to accusing her of being unworthy of her calling. Her eyes narrowed, and her hand brushed against her robe as though reassuring herself about her position. The accusation had, for a moment, stopped her.

"I cannot trust the word of anyone dealing with dark magic."

She had an answer for everything, of course. Honoria had always known The Truth in ways the rest of humanity apparently could only glimpse. As far as Mica could tell, she had never admitted to any mistake she might have made. Honoria simply never saw them. She had gone to the temple as a seeker at the age of fourteen, not even two years after their parent's death. Eight years later she was already headed into the mandatory ten years of seclusion within the temple before she could take her final vows. The ten years had not changed her attitude towards Mica.

From the look on Gregorian's face, he was preparing to say something which would not help because nothing ever did, and the confrontation would simply grow louder. Mica put a hand on his older brother's shoulder, stopping the outburst. They were already drawing too much attention. Servants and a couple clerks, still holding to quills and parchments, had gathered at both ends of the halls along with the guard who must have been stationed at the end opposite of Merriweather's post. The onlookers whispered like a distant hive of bees. Honoria had said many things that were no doubt going to make Mica's life more difficult, and if he stood here while she began to rage again, he might not keep his own anger in check.

"I am leaving," he said. "Gregorian, I caught nothing but a bit of surprise right at the end. I might be able to piece together more. There is no reason for me to stay."

Gregorian turned to him, scowling at first but then he gave way with a nod of agreement. "Yes. Thank you for arriving so promptly."

The servants scattered. As much as they liked a good show, they wouldn't want to be caught up in a disagreement between Prince Raventower and Priestess Raventower any more than Mica wanted to be here. Mica kept his own pace steady despite a developing headache that came both from the interaction with the dead and from his sister's interference. He had broken the connection to the dead man too quickly, and the tendrils of ice still jabbed at his arm like little needles. Mica rubbed his fingers of his right hand despite knowing it wouldn't help. He wanted to get home and rest.

The thought of home drew him on while each heartbeat echoed with a pounding in his head. He kept his eyes on the floor which seemed to be moving in slight undulations. He'd had this reaction to contact with the dead before and knew he had to get to the carriage where he could rest.

The wall moved to his right and in the next heartbeat, he saw a flash of metal in a pale hand.

Blade. Dark cloak.

Someone attacking him!

Mica reacted instinctively, kicking towards the groin as a blade caught his right arm. The attacker grunted but kept his head bowed and hidden in the shadows of a dark cloak.

Didn't want to be seen.

Mica grabbed at the cloth, but someone else grabbed him by his wounded arm. Stupid! He should have looked for another --

The second attacker had spun him half around. Mica saw hope of survival at that moment; Merriweather came around the corner of the hall with his cloak in hand which he'd forgotten it in his haste to escape from his sister. The lieutenant dropped the garment and gave a quick whistle that Mica knew would draw every guard in the area.

His attackers released him and ran.

Mica went to his knees.

ABOUT THE AUTHOR:

Hello!

I am an eclectic and prolific author who publishes in many genres, including Contemporary Fantasy, Epic Fantasy, Science Fiction, Mystery and Young Adult adventures. While I started on the outer edges of traditional publication with sales to small press and magazine publishers, I have since moved most of my work to the Indie world, and I am madly in love with the new era of publishing and the direct contact with readers. Feel free to write me!

I live in Nebraska with my husband, my cats, and a small but entirely useless dog.

Connect with Zette:
Web Site: http://lazette.net
Facebook: http://www.facebook.com/lazette.gifford
Joyously Prolific Blog: http://zette.blogspot.com/
(This one has weekly flash fiction stories)

www.ingramcontent.com/pod-product-compliance
Lightning Source LLC
Chambersburg PA
CBHW060536260626
47161CB00003B/929